IN GOD

WE TRUST

LOUISE GALVESTON

Special thanks to
Michelle Brown

razor
bill
An Imprint of Penguin Random House

A division of Penguin Young Readers Group
Published by the Penguin Group
Penguin Group (USA) LLC
345 Hudson Street
New York, New York 10014

USA / Canada / UK / Ireland / Australia / New Zealand /
India / South Africa / China
Penguin.com
A Penguin Random House Company

ISBN: 978-1-59514-679-3

Printed in the United States of America

1 3 5 7 9 10 8 6 4 2

For Dad and Mom:
Thanks for blazing such a bright trail for me.

CHAPTER 1
LEWIS

Our scouting party cautiously crossed the border of Toddlandia, exiting Todd's closet to wade through the Fiber Forest to the huge shriveled mass that once was round, smooth, and red. I was eager to understand the message Great Todd had left us, which was now turning wrinkled and spongy, its two green leaves withering on its stem. Not all of my friends agreed that the offensive object was meant to tell us something. But I believed the all-wise Todd did nothing by chance.

Persephone had sighted the Red Thing near the Refuse Dome shortly after we were returned to Toddlandia following the reign of terror by the Great Todd's evil classmate, Max Loving. My friend Herman, who had recently been elected mayor of Toddlandia, had taken an exploring party of some of the younger Toddlians to see if His Greatness had perhaps left some dirty clothes behind. For some reason, which I hoped studying the Red Thing might help us to understand, Todd had not been leaving us food in his closet lately.

At first we assumed the Red Thing was a gift from Todd, meant for us to play upon and explore. We swung from its thick brown stem, slid down its slick scarlet sides, and played hide-and-seek in its shadows. We even harvested some of its lovely, shiny skin to use as wallpaper for our dwellings, exposing a bright white interior, which amazingly, after a few minutes, turned to brown. What a magical thing Todd had bestowed upon us! Being something of an artist, I also spent several pleasant hours painting it from various angles.

But over time the Red Thing had ceased to be an object of fun and beauty. In fact, recently it had begun giving off an offensive odor. A white, fuzzy substance had started growing around the stem, and where the skin had been removed, the brown surface turned black and squished between one's toes. All this had led Mayor Herman to proclaim with "scientific certainty" that the Red Thing was indeed *rotten.*

This very morning, while the Great Todd was getting ready for school, I thanked him for his gift, telling him how much pleasure it had given us. I then suggested very gently that he might want to remove the Red Thing, since it now stank. His response was a curt "You ever think I might have *meant* to leave it there? Huh?" (In his defense I must say that he was in an unusual hurry and somewhat cross from having broken a shoelace *and* spilled Dr Pepper on his English homework. He seems to always be in a terrible hurry these days.)

Lesson to Lewis: leave His Greatness alone before he sets out on his journey to the fearsome place called Middle School. But when else could I speak on behalf of our people? Even I, loyal Toddlian that I am, see that our ruler has little time for us anymore. We are often left alone until late at night when Great Todd returns from the Mall. Whatever a Mall is, it must be an enchanted kingdom, for he is constantly asking his mother to transport him and Duddy there. Rarely upon return does he even remember to fling us his sweaty socks or grunge-encrusted gym clothes. I would be grateful if he would only fling me a friendly "Good night, Lew," the way he used to.

"Halfway there, friends," Herman panted as he pushed the fibers in front of him aside. "The stench grows stronger!"

Persephone pulled off her cowboy hat and wiped her brow. "If this ain't the most goldurned ridiculous waste of energy! I ask ya, Lew, has Todd ever left us some kind of secret code to cipher? If he wants to get somethin' off his chest, he says it right out."

Some of the others grunted in agreement.

But Herman shook his head. "Not necessarily. We must remember that the Powerful One's ways are not our ways. He is most awesome and perhaps, like a dutiful parent (insofar as I understand parenting), he desires to teach us by a system of rewards and punishments."

"Ooooo," chorused the other Toddlians.

Persephone crossed her arms and muttered, "Rewards and punishments? What are we, a bunch of unbroke broncos?"

"Perhaps," Herman said, "we need to consider *our* ways and not presume to know more than our Supreme Ruler. In the words of Albert Einstein, 'A true genius admits that he/she knows nothing.' "

More "ooo"s and some applause.

Persephone sighed and shimmied up a carpet fiber to "get a look-see."

"Well, we're nearly there, amigos," she said. "Though we'da been there and back if we'da rode the crickets I wrangled."

"You know how I feel about crickets, Persephone," I reminded her quietly.

"I have an idea," Herman huffed as we approached the rotten Red Thing. "What if we offer a tribute to Todd to show him we appreciate his care and leadership? Like the ancient Romans did to pacify their gods?"

Persephone stopped walking and turned to Herman. "Are you sayin' we should sacrifice fleas and such?

'Cause fer one thing, it sounds purty messy, and fer the other, I don't think he'd appreciate it much."

I shuddered. "Certainly you don't mean *that* kind of tribute, Herman?"

Herman rolled his eyes. "Of course not! I meant we could perform deeds of kindness."

We were close to the Refuse Dome now, which was an enormous white cylinder with a rounded top where Todd kept things he no longer wanted. The objects within were somewhat fascinating to us Toddlians, but unfortunately the slick white sides were very difficult to climb. The sickly-sweet stench of the Red Thing was so overpowering we held our noses.

"Deeds of kindness!" Persephone exclaimed. "We did Todd's computer homework jest last week. I had a dadgum charley horse fer three days from jumpin' all over the keyboard."

"Very noble of you, indeed," Herman said. Todd's Erector set was next to the Refuse Dome, and Herman slowly scaled a crane. "But let us pause to discuss this. I was thinking of something a little more formal." He stopped climbing, cupped his hands around his mouth, and addressed the Toddlian crowd below. "My fellow citizens, no doubt you have noticed that our beloved home, Toddlandia, is in a state of rapid decline."

I heard a groan behind me. "Do we have to do this now?" shouted Jasper, an adolescent Toddlian who often seemed to be in poor humor. "I thought we were checking out the Red Thing!"

Herman fixed him with a glare. "The message of the Red Thing is meaningless, unless we know how we will respond," he said.

Near the front of the crowd, Gerald, the eldest among us, nodded. "Mayor Herman is correct," he said in a grave voice. "Our leader has not been caring for us as he promised to, after the incident at the fair."

Jasper scoffed. "Sheesh, I'm just happy I haven't broken any limbs since we stopped training for that stupid carnival 'circus'!"

Mayor Herman shook his head. "It may be true that we haven't suffered the degradation of being forced to perform in some kind of sideshow attraction," he said, "but the Great Todd has not been as attentive as he might be."

My fellow Toddlians murmured, nodding their heads. "And it's a cryin' shame!" Persephone shouted above the rest.

"For example," Herman went on, "the drought we suffered this week when Lake Parkay dried up." He motioned toward the swimming hole at the bottom of the closet. We'd named it after the brand of margarine advertised on the container. "We nearly perished of thirst before Todd remembered to replenish our water supply."

The Toddlians grunted their agreement, growing more agitated.

"And what about the break-dancing lessons we were promised?" young Chester yelled. "Todd told us more than once he'd teach us how to do the Robot and the Worm!"

"We want the Worm!" screamed a particularly passionate Toddlian.

"We want the Worm!" chanted the rest of the crowd.

I signaled to Herman to calm the rabble-rousers. He made a slashing motion, and the Toddlians settled themselves. Herman climbed down from the crane, and we carefully approached the Red Thing.

I hadn't seen our former playground up close in its rotten state. How could anything once so shiny and round become so dull and slumped? I bent my head back, searching the Thing's wrinkled skin for clues as to why Todd had cursed it.

It looked as though he had taken one bite of the Thing before leaving it for us. The rust-colored skin was curled around angry-looking teeth marks exposing brown, slimy flesh. Was this a sign that Todd had tired of us, too? Were we being tossed aside for a more exciting civilization, perhaps one that lived in the glorious kingdom of the Mall?

What a horrible thought! "Maybe someone should climb on top for a better view," I suggested, wiping my burning eyes.

Persephone, being the bravest among us, volunteered to make the climb. She lassoed the white fuzzy stem and hoisted herself into the crevice of the first wrinkle. "This Thing's squishier 'n a slug's belly!" she called, pulling her bandana up over her nose. "Smells worse than skunk sweat, too. Shoo*wee*!"

We watched breathlessly as Persephone scaled the bumpy surface. Several times she lost her grip and slid, stopping herself from falling with the spurs on her heels.

"What do you see?" Herman called.

"A whole buncha nothin'," Persephone called back. "I'm heading back down; we've seen all there is to see here, which is naught. This smell's enough to make me blow my beans." She put her hand in a hole and started to scale back down. "Fool's errand if ever there was one," she muttered, looking for a foothold below her.

"What's that?" someone shrieked. Persephone saw it at the same time as the rest of us. A wriggling, slimy white creature popped out of the very hole where she had her hand. I felt my heart seize as I realized how horribly the younglings' demand for "the worm" had been answered—indeed, this terrible beast appeared to be exactly that.

Persephone let out a shriek and yanked her hand out of the wormhole, losing her grip. I rushed to catch her as she fell, but was blocked by the crowd, which was quickly becoming a boiling mess of mayhem. "I'm all right!" I heard her yell above the noise.

I glanced up at the worm again. Its eyeless, ghostly

white body was weaving back and forth, as if to defy anyone else to come near the Red Thing.

Chester let out a bloodcurdling scream. "Great Todd, we didn't mean it!" he cried. "We didn't want this kind of worm!"

"Have mercy on us, Great Todd!" was the cry on everyone's lips as they stampeded back toward the safety of Toddlandia. But of course, Todd was nowhere to be found—like usual lately.

I joined Persephone in the panicked throng, and together we looked about for Herman. Finally I recognized his faint cries above the din of confusion.

We sprinted back to the Red Thing. *We must save Herman!*

"Help!" he whimpered pitifully. "Is anyone out there?"

"Take courage!" I answered. "Where are you?"

"Near the Refuse Dome," he moaned. "Please . . . hurry!"

I followed his voice and found him crumpled in a heap at the base of the Refuse Dome's curved wall. "Trampled in the stampede," he said through clenched teeth. "I fear . . . for my tibia bone."

His left ankle was swollen and already turning a gruesome green. "Let's hope it's merely sprained," I said. "Can you put your arm around my shoulder?"

He nodded, and together we hobbled in the direction

of Toddlandia. I wished I had given in and ridden a cricket, for Herman's sake. "There can be no argument now," he said solemnly. "Todd left the Red Thing and its revolting resident as a form of *punishment*. We have angered him yet again and have incurred his wrath."

"Sssshh!" I commanded. "Your pain is making you downhearted. Remember how many times Todd has protected our people from danger! Why would he turn on us now?"

Herman grew fatigued. We stopped to let him rest, and he raised his eyes to mine. "You forget that his reasoning is far different from ours."

"Todd is my *friend*," I protested. "Why would he be so cruel?"

He grimaced and took a deep breath. "Todd is not your friend, Lewis. He's your *god*. And an angry one at that."

My heart sank within me. "But can't he be both?"

CHAPTER 2

A big hunk of blueberry bagel fell onto my shirt, and I swatted it off, only to notice something weird. *Holy frijoles!* Where was my collar? I looked over my shoulder, and sure enough, I had my shirt on backward! I had to get it turned around before she—before *anyone*—came into class.

Mr. Katcher's office door was open, so I snuck inside and clicked it closed. I almost set the bagel on a stack of funky-smelling plastic bags, until I looked closer and saw they were full of dead frogs. *Gagadocious.* I held the bagel with my teeth and spun the shirt around so Koi Boy was facing forward. Now if I could only get my *head* on straight. I still felt like I had when I left the house this morning: half asleep.

That's what I got for getting up thirty minutes early so I could stop by Dale's Deli and stand outside for ages, watching for *her*. I'd actually *showered* and everything. Which kind of backfired, because my hair was wet, and it was freezing out.

I'd waited, teeth chattering and hair still dripping, as long as I could without being late for first period. Finally I arrived at the sad conclusion that Charity Driscoll wasn't actually coming to the deli that morning, so I dashed inside and bought a bagel, since I'd skipped breakfast to get there so early. I was too jittered up to think about asking for cream cheese.

I muscled down another bite. Like the bagel, my brilliant scheme had a hole in it.

I strolled out of Katcher's office and headed to the sink on the back wall for a drink of water. I gulped down a big mouthful, feeling guilty as I remembered that in my rush to leave the house this morning I'd forgotten to refill Lake Parkay for the Toddlians. Hopefully they weren't super thirsty. I'd make it up to them this afternoon by giving them a sip of my Dr Pepper.

Did my shirt smell like formaldehyde? I sniffed it just in case. Nope. Nothing but Dad's Old Spice.

"Yeah, Buttrock, you really stink!" an all-too-familiar voice blared in my ear. "I'll take that off your hands." Max Loving helped himself to what was left of my bagel.

"Good morning to you too, Max," I said dryly.

Totally invading my personal space, Max backed me into the corner where Mr. Bone Jangles, the life-size skeleton, hung. "Oh, it's not a good morning. Not for me, not for you, and especially not for your little buggy buddies."

My gut clenched around the half-eaten bagel. Max hadn't even mentioned the Toddlians to me for a couple of weeks—ever since we humiliated him by scaring him snotless when he came to my house to try to take my skateboard. I'd once thought Max was the coolest kid at Wakefield Middle School, but I quickly learned he was just the biggest bully. Even his henchmen, eighth graders Spud and Dick, seemed to have dumped him after the whole skateboard debacle. What was he after *now*?

Max was breathing heavy and starting to foam around the lips like a mad dog. He shoved me right into the skeleton. The plastic bones rattled, and Mr. Jangles's leg fell off. Max picked up the femur and thumped my chest with it.

"You and those little buggers cost me my Xbox." *Thump, thump.* "And I had to borrow the hundred bucks the fair fined me from my parents, who are making me pay back every penny." He shoved a meaty finger into my chest. "If you and your dorkwad friends hadn't ruined my Flea Circus Redux by switching your bug people with those ants, I'd have made enough for an Xbox and then some."

Was he expecting me to feel sorry for him after he put the Toddlians through weeks of cruel circus-stunt training, nearly killing them? It had taken me too long to figure out that Max was using our joint science project, a Toddlian circus, as an excuse to hurt the Toddlians, but as soon as I did, I hatched a scheme to stop him and save the little guys. Clearly, Max still hadn't forgiven me for the fallout. But what could I say? I wasn't afraid of him anymore. "Sorry, Max."

His beady eyes disappeared under his unibrow. "Oh, you will be, Buttrock." *Thump, thump.* He tossed poor Mr. Bone Jangles's femur down on the counter. "You will be."

I glanced toward the door. Kids were starting to trickle in. "I don't know why you're still so mad at me. You ended up getting a good grade on the science test anyway, so your parents aren't sending you to military school."

Max snorted. "Yeah, but now we have to do that stupid makeup science project for Katcher."

I frowned at him. "Now?" I asked. Mr. Katcher had given us both Fs on the failed Toddlian circus. *But* he'd also offered us the opportunity to do makeup projects. The only thing was . . . "They're due by Friday, Max." I'd spent the last two weeks researching scientific urban legends and had finally handed in my paper the day before. "Shouldn't you be nearly done by now?"

Max growled at me. Actually *growled.* "Yeah, well, it seems I have to pull together a project real quick," he muttered, grabbing the femur off the counter and jabbing it into my ribs again. "I was trying to teach my sister's hamster to squeak when I rang a bell, but there was an . . . accident."

Don't ask. Don't ask. "That's too bad, Max."

He shoved a sausagey finger into my nose. *Ugh.* His fingernails were filthy. "So I figured you could give me your project," he said. "Or else."

If this had happened a few weeks ago, I would have peed my pants in terror. Now, all I felt was annoyed . . . and kind of relieved that I had an easy answer for him. "Oh, too bad, Max. I turned my project in yesterday."

Max's dark eyes turned black for a second as fury flashed across his face. But he quickly recovered, giving me a slow grin. "Oh, that's too bad, Buttrock. I guess that means I need something I can pull into a project really fast. Maybe a new scientific discovery, something nobody's ever seen before? Hmmm . . ."

I didn't like where this was going. "If you're talking about the Toddlians, Max, you already tried to use them as your science project, and it was a disaster, remember?"

Max glared at me. "It was a disaster because your nerdy friend stole them before we could show them to Mr. Katcher," he hissed. He meant Lucy, my homeschooled neighbor and sort-of assistant in caring for the Toddlians. Man, his breath was terrible. "If he actually saw them, I know I'd get an A. Plus . . ." He grinned that smarmy grin again. "I'd get the *pleasure* of *playing* with your little bug people some more. Hey—do you think they'd squeal when I rang a bell? I bet I could make 'em. HA!"

Gulp. I hadn't been scared of Max five minutes ago, but now my heart was pounding in my chest. He might be a stupid bully—but I totally believed he was capable of hurting the Toddlians. Heck, I'd seen him do it.

"You can't have them," I said pointedly, then feinted left and tried to make a break for my desk.

But Max blocked my escape with the plastic bone. "Not so fast, bug boy. If you won't give 'em to me, I'm comin' to collect."

Don't be afraid of him. Don't be afraid. He's not going to just come to my house and take them, right? He's just a bully with bad breath. "Collect?" I asked, and it came out in a squeaky tone that probably sounded a lot like Max's sister's poor hamster.

He pressed his forehead into mine and spat, "Sleep with one eye open, Buttrock. I know where you live, and I'm gonna tear your tiny friends limb from little limb."

Max gave me one last thump and hooked the femur back to the rest of the leg just as Mr. Katcher and the rest of the kids came through the door.

I beat it to the back of the lab, taking my seat next to Duddy, who was chatting with Ernie Buchenwald. It was still weird to think that my best bud and Ernie were friends. Back in elementary school, Ernie had been our nemesis. But then he and Duddy had done their science project together and bonded over a shared passion for ants.

"'Thup, Todd?" Ernie greeted me, nodding his orange-Brillo-topped head at me. Ernie wore the Mother of All Retainers, and as he nodded a bit of drool dripped down onto Duddy's desk.

Duddy signaled toward Max with a nod. "You okay?" he whispered. "What did that meathead want?"

"Nothing," I muttered. I didn't want to get into it, and besides, I refused to believe that Max could actually sneak into my house and steal the Toddlians.

Duddy mimicked Max's glare, then crossed his eyes and said, "Durrrr."

"HAW HAW HAW," Ernie laughed. Just then the bell rang, and Mr. Katcher hopped up onto his cluttered desk, shooting Ernie a warning look that sent him scuttling back to his desk at the end of our row. Mr. Katcher picked up a big beaker full of a light brown foamy liquid and drank it down. Was that his *coffee*?

"Today, my future Nobel Prize winners," he said, setting down the near-empty beaker, "we're going to talk about volume. Not volume as in how many decibels can I

turn up my heavy metal before my eardrums rupture"—
he jumped off the desk and played an air guitar while
banging his head—"but volume as in how much salted
caramel latte did Mr. Katcher just drink?" He wriggled
his eyebrows and twisted one end of his brown mustache like a cartoon villain.

I had no idea what kind of high-powered caffeine
was in that stuff, but I hoped the Toddlians never got
hold of any.

Mr. Katcher pulled out a two-liter container of
Mountain Dew from under his desk, shook it hard, and
asked, "Which of you young geniuses cares to tell me
how many milliliters are in this? Correct answer gets
the prize."

Hands shot up all over the room. Mr. Katcher's mustache danced as he consulted his clipboard. At last he
said, "Miss Driscoll, would you honor us with your
answer?"

We all turned to look at Charity Driscoll, and my
heart felt like it squeezed into my throat. As she nodded
her head, causing her long, golden-brown hair to ripple
like a shiny waterfall, I totally forgave her for not stopping by the deli this morning, robbing me of the chance
to try and chat her up. Charity had moved with her family from Florida a week before, and she was by far the
prettiest girl I'd ever seen.

Charity slid gracefully out of her seat in the front

row and turned to face the class. "One liter equals one thousand milliliters, therefore that two-liter contains two thousand milliliters." Even her voice was sweet as honey. I could have listened to it all day . . .

Mr. Katcher handed the bottle to her and bowed. "Well done, Miss Driscoll." He coughed. "Er, be careful opening that up, okay?"

Charity gave him a big smile and handed the two-liter back. "That's okay, Mr. Katcher. I prefer Dr Pepper."

My mouth dropped open, but I quickly slammed it shut before anyone saw me catching flies. What were the chances? *I* preferred Dr Pepper too! Maybe we could have talked about that if she'd stopped by Dale's that morning. Not that I ever seemed to know what to say to her. I'd probably just have stood there like a goggle-eyed mouth breather, as usual.

I watched her now, my heart pounding. If only I could get her to look at me with those aqua eyes. They were the same blue as the Fernsopian pool that Varusa the Lizard Queen rose out of in *Dragon Sensei*.

But I wasn't alone in my crush on Charity. While Mr. Katcher stepped into his office to get a bunch more beakers, two other admirers leaned over to try their lines on her.

Max, flexing a bicep: "Hey, Char-Char, how many milliwhatevers are in this baby?"

Rudy Reyes, a freckled kid who usually kept to

himself, suddenly dropped to one knee. "Liters of Dew—
you have two—one for me, one for you. Come now,
baby, why be shy? In my bag is an extra MoonPie! Eat
lunch with me?"

The whole class groaned at that, but even these
lame-o lines made my heart sink. These guys might
have tanked, but at least they were brave enough to talk
to Charity. What kind of chance did *I* have? I couldn't
string two words together when she was around.

Jordan Pelinski, who was famous for eating and then
puking up an entire one-pound bag of Skittles at Cub
Scout camp, had just finished serenading Charity with
"My Girl" when Mr. Katcher came back into the room,
his arms overflowing with tubes and beakers. "Let's
get to the business at hand, shall we, ladies and gents?
Speaking of hands, lend me some."

A couple of kids helped him set the containers on a
table and fill them with water. Charity offered to drip
drops of food coloring into the beakers. Her hair gleamed
in the morning sunlight like liquid gold. *Oooh, that's
nice. That would be a good line to use on her, if I ever
muster the guts.*

Charity finished her job and walked slowly toward
her desk. Was she looking at *me*? Before I could do
anything stupid, like wink at her, I heard Paul Mosely
chuckle behind me. *Oh, of course.* She'd been aiming that smile at *him*. After all, he was only the best
basketball player in sixth grade, and had straight white

teeth with no braces, like something out of a toothpaste commercial.

I felt myself crumple a little bit and had to look away. *Who am I kidding?* Charity could get any guy at Wakefield Middle School. She would never give me a second glance. I'd have to do a lot more than bump into Charity at a bagel shop or the mall to get her attention.

I glanced across the aisle to my best friend, wondering if Duddy might hold the answer to my romantic woes. After all, *he* thought I was pretty cool. (And before the Toddlians, he might have been the only one to think that besides my immediate family.) He was wiggling a triangle-folded note at me, his blond bowl-cut bangs quivering as he gave me a mini Saki Salute. I couldn't help smiling. Duddy might not know what I wanted, but he always knew what I needed. *Distraction.* The signal meant that he thought we should do a little *Dragon Sensei* duel on paper.

Mr. Katcher's back was still turned to us, so Duddy slid the note to me with his shoe. He'd drawn Mongee-Poo, Koi Boy's green monkey sidekick, hurling a flaming poo grenade. The bubble coming out of his mouth said, "hoo hoo hi-yah! hahaha, oora, i'm gonna poo ya!" That was straight out of the latest episode of *Dragon Sensei,* "The Poo's on You!," in which Koi Boy and Mongee-Poo take revenge on pretty much every villain in the entire series.

I shot Duddy a thumbs-up then scribbled Emperor

Oora, Giant Salamander of All Evilness, saying, "Face it, Koi Boy, Fernsopi shall be mine! You and your foul, furry friend here should return to that clown who calls himself the Dragon Sensei and—" That's as far as I got before a hairy hand snatched the paper out from under my pen.

Mr. Katcher cleared his throat. "Hmm. A green primate and some sort of robed reptile. Gentlemen, what *is* this?" He read the note in a deadpan voice. Even I have to admit, it did sound stupid.

Max sure thought so. He nearly busted a gut guffawing. When he finally caught his breath he said, "I know what it is, Mr. Katcher! It's from *Dragon Sensor*, that baby anime junk Buttrock and Scanlon are always playing! HOO HOO HI-YAH HAHAHA!"

The rest of the class cracked up. Whether they really thought it was funny or were just afraid of Max, I didn't know. I *did* know that Charity whirled around in her seat, staring at me with wide eyes.

Great. I'd finally gotten her to realize that I exist, only to horrify her with my dorkdom.

My face felt like lava, and I seriously considered faking sick so I could spend the rest of the day holed up at home, wallowing in my stupidity. But that was the way of wusses, and if I'd learned anything lately, it was to face my humiliation head on.

Mr. Katcher let us off with a lecture but said the next note would land us in KP. KP was short for Katcher

Patrol and was a million times worse than detention. You had to clean all the tools and trays from dissection, scrub out moldy petri dishes, clean up Camo the chameleon's lizard poop, and do whatever other disgusting jobs Mr. Katcher felt like making you do.

We measured the colored water in the beakers for the rest of the hour. When the bell rang, I tried to slink out of the room without running into Charity, but being the talented klutz that I am, I dropped my *Dragon Sensei* notebook right beside her desk. As I grabbed it I couldn't help glancing at her.

She was looking right at me, her head tilted and eyebrows raised. There was a hint of a smile at the corners of her mouth. I stood there, frozen, until she gave me a little nod. That broke the spell. I stumbled into the hallway half-embarrassed, half-enraptured.

She'd nodded. At me!

Did that mean I might actually have a chance?

CHAPTER 3

I grabbed my tray of chicken wads and tots and scooted onto the bench across the table from Duddy and Ernie. Duddy was all riled up about something and gulped down a mouthful of food, then chased it with chocolate milk.

"Todd! Didja hear the—*buuuuuurp*—news?" He was so excited he didn't even laugh at his own burp, which was very unlike Duddy.

I stabbed a chicken wad and drowned it in ketchup. "No, Dudster. I have no—wait! Have they released the Lizard Queen action figure?" I'd gotten my mom to agree to drive me to the mall the second it came out, in exchange for handling my sister Daisy's baths for a week, so if it was out, I definitely wanted to know.

Duddy shook his head. "No! Three spots just opened up on the swim team!" He waited for my reaction.

"Uhhhh . . . okay." I just raised an eyebrow. "You have a chocolate mustache."

Duddy licked off the mustache and tried again. "Tell him, Ernie."

I looked over at our former nemesis. "What's going on with the swim team?"

Ernie cleared his throat, putting down his liverwurst-and-onion sandwich. "Ith called the *WAVETH*, acthually," he said, nearly knocking me over with his terrible-smelling breath.

"The WAVES?" I tried to breathe through my mouth as I chomped on a tot.

Ernie nodded. "Yeah, the Wakefield WAVETH. It thtandth for thomething. Erm . . . We Are . . . Very Excellent . . . Thwimmers. Or thomething."

I had to laugh. "Ernie, come on."

Duddy broke in. "Listen, though! Ernie knows what he's talking about. The swimmers who got kicked off were Ernie himself and some seventh grade girl named Cassandra and her friend Francesca—least I think that's what he said."

"That'th right." Ernie adjusted his retainer with his

tongue. "Catttttthhhhhaaaandra ith amathing. The'th like . . ." He looked off toward the window, and his eyes went soft. I glanced at Duddy, but he was watching Ernie intently. "Imathine the prettieth girl you've ever theen."

The prettiest girl you've ever seen. I thought of Charity's golden-waterfall hair and pool-blue eyes. Was Cassandra as pretty as Charity? Was that even possible? "So you like her?" I asked. It was weird to think about Ernie Buchenwald, former Swirlie Overlord and Not Super-Sensitive Guy, having a crush on anyone.

But now he sighed pensively. "Ith not juth a cruth. I think Catttttthhhaaaandra ith my thoul mate."

"Your thoul—eh, soul mate?" I echoed. This time I caught Duddy's eye, and he shot me an *I can't believe it either* look.

"Ern, get to the part about the WAVES," he prodded.

Ernie chuckled, sending little bits of liverwurst flying everywhere. "Well, it wath delightful. Cattttthhaaaandra really bringth out my playful thide. What we did wath, we put Palmolive dith thoap in the pool filterth, and the entire pool building wath filled with thudth!" He made a big mountain with his hands, smiling dreamily. "It wath awethome."

That actually sounded kind of cool. "Man, I wish I'd been there!"

Ernie nodded. "It wath all Catttttthaaaandra'th idea." He took a sip of milk and then sighed. "The'th a real firecracker."

Duddy looked at me. "So whaddaya wanna do?"

"About what?"

"The swim team!"

I just looked at him. "What's there to do?"

"*Try out!* Duh!"

I snorted. "Are you kidding? It's not like either one of us is the next Michael Phelps. I hate to break this to ya, Dudman, but we aren't exactly jock material."

Duddy puffed out his practically nonexistent chest. "Speak for yourself, Butroche. But seriously, there's this real old rule at WMS that if you go out for a sport you don't have to take gym."

He had my attention. "Yeah?"

Ernie nodded. "Yeah. It'th true. It'th the one bad thing about getting kicked off. Catttthhhaaaaandra'th trying to get uth on the badminton team tho we can thtill thkip gym."

Duddy poked my shoulder. "It gets even better, Todd. You get to take fun electives instead, like art and drama and stuff."

I took a swig of milk. *No gym?* That meant no more shower-time humiliation, no more Icy Hot in my undies . . . Just last week Max had used gym class as an opportunity to give me the mother of all supersonic wedgies. I was still raw from the rash.

I nodded at Duddy. "You had me at *no more gym*."

Duddy grinned. "Great! Plus, Madame Dauphinee, the French teacher, makes crêpes for the entire team after every meet, whether they win or lose!" He pumped his fist in the air. *"Vive la France!"*

"Uh, did you say she makes 'creeps' for everyone?" I'd had enough of those, thank you very much.

Ernie chuckled, showering us with more liverwurst. "Not creepth . . . *craaapeth!* You never had one? They're like thin pancaketh thmothered in awethome thauthe!"

I sucked a Jell-O square through my straw and smiled, squirting red goo between my teeth. "Gentlemen, you've sold me. We have to do this!"

"Awesome! It's on!" Duddy and I high-fived each other, and then Ernie. Suddenly Duddy frowned, like something had just occurred to him. "Um, Todd, can you swim?"

"Of course I can!" But Duddy was nodding really slowly, and it set something off in my brain. I had tons of pictures of the Dudster and me at the beach as kids, and in each one, Duddy was wearing bright orange inflatable "swimmies" on each arm. "Dud—you can swim too, right?"

He just shrugged and took another swig of chocolate milk. "I'll figure something out."

Our conversation was cut short by a ruckus over at the eighth graders' tables. A food fight was in full force. I stopped chewing my chicken wad to watch.

"Miss it?" Duddy asked quietly.

I thought back to those few glorious days when I was part of the Zoo Crew, Max's gang of cool kids, wildly slinging Ring Dings as Max's right-hand man. It had been nice . . . but it had nearly cost me my best friend, and the Toddlians.

"Naw," I said. Even Max wasn't allowed to sit with the Zoo Crew anymore. Ever since the Toddlians had humiliated him on my skateboard, Max ate his lunch a couple of tables away with Hank Fiddlehead and Joey Dupree, two lower-level sixth grade bullies from Newton Elementary.

When I looked back up at the Zoo Crew table, Charity was sashaying past. The tot tossing stopped while those guys called to Charity, trying to charm her into sitting with them. She paused like she was thinking about it.

Okay, so maybe there *was* something to being popular.

But then she kept moving, walking by Max, Hank, and Joey. Max shoved a guy over and motioned for Charity to sit by him, but she shook her head and kept walking.

Right. Toward. Me.

I couldn't believe it. Her tight smile burst into a gleaming grin as she nodded at me again and crossed the cafeteria. The whole thing seemed to be happening in slow motion, her golden-brown hair swishing around her shoulders, her ocean-blue eyes locked onto mine . . . shoot, even the veggie burger on her tray looked edible in her reflected glory.

It was exactly like the scene where Varusa, the Lizard

Queen, emerges slowly out of the Pool of Secrets. In fact, I thought I heard the beautiful violin melody that the show used as Varusa's theme music.

I came crashing back to reality when Charity stopped beside me and said, "Hey! So you and your friend watch *Dragon Sensei*?"

My mouth opened but no sound came out. It didn't matter, because Duddy started talking enough for the both of us. "Watch it? We're the founders of the Koi Boy Karate Choppers, and we basically role-play nonstop. You should see our costumes! Todd's Oora robe actually has Boom Shrooms that blow green smoke and—"

"Shuddup!" Max bellowed behind Charity. I hadn't noticed him trailing her from his table. She set her tray down and sat on my left. Sweet heat shot through me. Charity was so close I could smell the coconuts in her shampoo. If she even noticed Max was there, she didn't show it.

"Hey!" Max protested. "You don't want to sit with these losers. They're first-class dorks, let me tell you. They waste all their time pretending to be bees or something." He leaned into her. "Can you believe that?"

Charity turned to me. "Does he mean Vespa the Vengeful, Hornet of Hate?"

Ohmygosh. She *knew*!

Good thing Duddy answered her, because there was a watermelon-sized lump in my throat. "You should see our friend Lucy's Vespa costume. It's got hologram wings and a neon stinger and everything."

She smiled at Duddy. "Vespa's too spiteful for my taste. Personally, I prefer to play the Lizard Queen. Varusa's my favorite Fernsopian female."

I couldn't speak. *Is this really happening?*

Max snorted incredulously, shook his head, and walked away.

Charity turned back to me and smiled. "You know, we absolutely *have* to get together and have a *Dragon Sensei* battle jam."

I think I died inside. But what a delicious death it was.

I must have gone to heaven because Charity reached over and squeezed my arm. "Let's make plans soon."

CHAPTER 4

PERSEPHONE

It weren't long after the Red Thing Fiasco that I shimmied up to Mount Bambino's summit, where Lewis was waiting to powwow. He stopped muttering to himself when he saw me, and I plopped my patootie down next to his.

"Thanks for meeting me here, Persephone," he said.

"Sure shootin'," I replied. "Whatcha doin' with that paper? More of Todd's schoolin', I reckon?"

Lewis shook his head and forked over the circles of paper he'd snatched from the funny thing Todd called a *hole punch*. They said:

Oh, Great Todd live forever etc. We, your loyal
subjects, are aware that you have many kingdoms
to rule: Middle School, The Mall, Fernsopi, and
Toddlandia. We also realize that you must manage
your odious homework when all the while defending
yourself against eighth graders. (Mention ever-
present evil of The Adorable One They Call Daisy
and her frequent raids on his room. Do not mention
your affection for her or the art lessons.) But if you
could spare a few moments of precious time for your
humble servant Lewis—

I couldn't tolerate it. I grabbed the papers and wadded them up, shaking my fist. "What kind of pig swill
is this, Lew? You gonna lick the dirt off his shoes while
yer at it? Have a mite of self-respect, hombre! You're not
figurin' on reading that to him, are you?"

"Well, no, not read it, exactly. These are just talking points to use as a guide. I'll speak straight from my
heart." Lewis shot me that goldurn darlin' lopsided grin
of his and put on his puppy-dog eyes. "I had hoped you
would accompany me to 'palaver' with His Toddness."

Blast it all! I never could say nay when he asked like
that. "Sure, Lew, I'll be your pardner." *Make ya stick to
yer guns, too, iffen ya start to turn lily-livered!* Not that I
believed for a second that Todd would *comprendo* what
Lewis was aiming at. Or even give a plug nickel.

I was still hotter than grease on a griddle about the rotten Red Thing and its creepy critter. Todd had made it clear as water in a rain barrel what he thought of us by leavin' the nasty rotten mess to skeer us half to death.

What had we done to deserve to be treated like we were lower than dirt? Not one dadgum thing. The thought of it boiled me over so bad I blurted out, "Don't know why we're wastin' our time on this sorry excuse for a god."

Lewis gasped. "Persephone, I beg you—"

But I wasn't ready to stop. "I'm sick as a sow's ear of your kowtowin' to Todd and getting nothin' for it but a smackdown."

"Blasphemy!" Lewis hissed, clapping a hand over my mouth. "I beseech you, stop this sacrilegious talk! Do you want to incur more of his wrath?"

He was shaking so much that I let it ride with "All righty, no need to get yer bloomers in a bundle! It's not like he can hear us. Cool yer heels, for cryin' out loud."

I said no more about it then, but the notion of a new leader gnawed at my mind aplenty.

When it was high time for Todd to be home, Lewis and I parked our patooties on top of his laptop computer—the one spot we knew he'd see us. But when he came in, Todd headed right to his desk and started riflin' around on the shelf above it.

"GREAT TODD, MAY YOU LIVE FOREVER!" Lewis stood and hollered. "May we have a word with you?"

"Just a minute, Lewis," Todd muttered. "I need to bone up on my *Dragon Sensei* this afternoon." He started layin' his fool dolls on the desk right next to us. "Koi Boy, Mongee-Poo . . . how'd these get out of order? Oora should be right here," he insisted. "Wait, where's Oora—AAAAHHH! WHO DID THIS TO OORA?!" He slammed the doll against the desk, causin' an earthquake that knocked Lewis clean over. I saw right away what had him all hopped up. The thing was missin' a leg.

Todd started foaming at the mouth like a rabid dog as he found another one of his figure thingies one-legged. He sank into his chair and plopped his noggin right on top of the computer—we jumped clear jest before his head hit, barely escaping with our hides!

"I don't believe this," Todd cried. "Is nothing safe?"

Lewis hustled up onto Todd's hand and made a beeline for his shoulder.

"Great Todd live forever," he began into Todd's ear. "I know you are busy, but might you spare a few seconds of your precious time—"

Todd lifted his head and grabbed the micro-glasses that Lucy had made, allowin' him to see us more clearly. He slid them on and waved at his dollies, moaning, "Have you guys seen these? How can I show my *Dragon Sensei* collection to Charity at school tomorrow when Saki and Oora are missing legs? I mean, sure, they regenerate limbs on TV, but this is real life, and I'm just . . . I can't . . ."

Lewis patted Todd on the cheek. "I am sorry, Your Greatness. Perhaps Persephone and I could help you look for the missing appendages, and then we could discuss—"

"But you must have seen who did this!" Todd said, wild-eyed. "Maybe Herman needed them for some invention, or the little Toddlians decided they wanted some slides for their playground . . ." He pointed his trigger finger at me. "Or you—you totally messed up my Lego set that one time. Did you turn them into jumps for cricket training?"

I pointed right back at him. "Before you go gettin' a burr under yer blanket, why don't you try talkin' to Daisy? That young Houdini's the real whodunit in this here situation!"

Todd threw his head back and howled, "DAAAISY!!!" without so much as a "sorry I acted like a ninny" to us.

Lewis picked hisself up from where he'd crashed onto the desk again and cleared his throat. "Great Todd, may I say in Daisy's defense that she only wanted the legs for artistic purposes? She meant nothing nefarious, I am sure of it. And I think even you would agree that her interpretation of 'Twinkle Twinkle Little Star' is a beautiful collage, much enhanced by the geometric angles of shapely salamander legs." Lew tried his lopsided grin on His Greatness, but it didn't work.

"You let her do it?" Todd asked, all stupefied. "You,

my own people, who are supposed to protect my possessions when I'm not here, let that demented toddler
waltz right in and wreck my favorite *Dragon Sensei* figures?" He shook his head and gave us the double stink-
eye. "I thought you were my friends."

I slung my arm around Lewis to support him as
Todd kicked his chair back, ripped off the glasses, and
stomped outta there, hollerin' "DAAAISY!" loud enough
to wake a dead rattlesnake.

Lewis looked at me with soggy eyes. I was plumb
torn in two, between feelin' his pain and wantin' to sic
Duddy's ants on Todd in his sleep. "Never you mind,"
I said, wipin' a stray tear from Lewis's cheek. "You
showed gumption and gave it a go. He'll most likely simmer down once he gets those legs back."

Lewis hiccupped. "And if he doesn't?"

I shrugged. "We'll have to break that bronc when we
get to it." I didn't bring up gettin' ourselves a better god
again. Not with Lew this low.

CHAPTER 5

"**D**AAAISY, WHERE ARE YOU!" I yelled as I entered the nursery. Daisy stood at her light-up music table with her back to me. She had "Old MacDonald" cranked to an ear-bloodying pitch. I was pretty sure she'd hacked the toy to make it demonically annoying, like herself. My sister might look like the angel Lewis depicted her as in the painting on my ceiling, but I knew that under those blond curls lurked the devious mind of an evil genius.

I hopped carefully through the minefield of blocks and baby Legos that she'd scattered across her floor, no doubt to cripple unwanted intruders. Squatting down beside her, I took a deep breath and tried to sweet-talk her, the way Mom did.

"Daisy," I said over the hideous high-pitched music. "Look at Toddy for a second."

Daisy turned and stared right at me, blinked twice, then very slowly and deliberately punched the duck button on top of her toy table. She then ignored me and wiggled her little hiney to the beat. "WITH A QUACK-QUACK HERE AND A QUACK-QUACK THERE . . ."

I wasn't giving up that easy. I waved the action figures in front of her face. "Toddy's dollies. See?"

Daisy ignored me, so I picked up Becky Burps-A-Lot and handed it to her. "*This* is Daisy's dolly." She grabbed the doll by the foot and flung it over her shoulder so hard it crashed against the opposite wall with a defeated *BUUURRP!* Grinning at me, she gleefully punched the cow button.

"EE-I-EE-I-OOOO! AND ON THAT FARM HE HAD A—"

"DAISY!" I barked, starting to lose it. "You are in *big* trouble, kiddo. LOOK AT ME, DAISY. WOULD YOU JUST SHUT THAT THING OFF FOR A SECOND AND LOOK AT ME?"

She jabbed the duck button. "WITH A QUACK-QUACK HERE AND A QUACK-QUACK THERE . . ."

"HAVE YOU SEEN THE LEGS TO THESE?" I shook Oora and Saki right in front of Daisy's nose, hard enough to send her little blond curl waving in the breeze. "TODD'S TOYS! NOT DAISY'S TOYS!"

Pig button. "WITH AN OINK-OINK HERE . . ."

The "OINK OINK"s finally sent me over the edge. I jumped up and threw my hands in the air. *You know what? You win!* I squealed, my voice as high as the pig's in the sadistic singing. "You win again! That's right! Just go into my room whenever you want, destroy my stuff, and because you're 'only a baby,' don't worry about ever getting punished."

Daisy blinked at me, as if to say, *You done?* Then she jabbed the horse button.

I felt something inside me break. "YOU KNOW WHAT THE WORST THING IS? I don't even get the satisfaction of chewing you out about it because YOU DON'T EVEN UNDERSTAND WHAT I'M SAYING!"

Daisy narrowed her eyes at me. "NEIGH-NEIGH HERE AND A NEIGH-NEIGH THERE—" She nodded her head in time to the music, still wiggling her rear end. Then she plugged the Binky into her mouth and noshed furiously. "Nom nom nom nom."

I shook my head and said what I'd heard Mom exclaim a million times: "I GIVE UP!"

Suddenly the doorbell rang, and my heart jumped up in my chest. Was it Charity? Had Duddy told her where I lived?

I picked my way as quickly as I could across the death trap that was Daisy's carpet. *BUUUUUUUURP* went the Becky doll as I stepped on her stomach in my hurry to get out of there. I flung myself at the door and pulled it open. It wasn't Charity.

Max Loving leaned against the doorframe.

A few minutes later I sat in the living room directly across from my mother's new piano student.

"Isn't it great, Todd?" my mom said. "Your friend Max was so inspired by Lucy's playing the last time he was over that he's decided to take piano lessons himself."

I nodded, trying to swallow the scream that was lodged in my throat.

"I told you I was coming to collect," Max mouthed.

That's when I spotted my mom's demon dog, Princess VanderPuff, nosing around her empty food dish. While my mom chatted Max up about his music preferences, I grabbed a cracker with peanut butter off the tray my mom had set out "for our guest" and held it down near my chair, smiling and trying to act natural. VanderPuff was on a diet and not supposed to have any human food (meaning food *for* humans, not food *made of* humans; she sure still enjoyed biting the heck out of ankles), but I needed to create a distraction so that I could leave the room and get to the Toddlians without Max noticing.

Demon Dog delicately sniffed the air and then locked eyes with me. I shook the cracker and then tossed it right between Max's huge sneakers. I turned back to my mom and Max, smiling as VanderPuff suddenly shot across the kitchen and launched herself at Max's feet. Startled, Max let out a yelp, shielding his feet with his meaty hands. Unsurprisingly, Demon Dog didn't like being separated from her cracker *at all,* so she sprung at Max and latched onto his calf like a bear trap.

Mua ha ha ha, I thought, glowing with satisfaction. *Success!*

"YOWCH!" Max was hollering, shaking his leg while Mom tried to pry the poodle loose.

"Help me, Todd!" Mom begged through gritted teeth.

"Bad dog," I said, arms crossed. I made a mental note to slip the beast my bacon tomorrow morning as I stood and muttered something about going to find one of VanderPuff's toys.

As soon as I was out of the kitchen, I escaped down the hallway to my room. I had to figure out somewhere to hide the tiny guys, quick!

I searched under my bed. There was a shoebox full of baseball cards. I dumped them onto my desk and threw open my closet door, then got on my knees and turned the box on its side. "Everyone get in!" I commanded. *"Now!"* But there was no movement. Where were they? I darted to the desk and grabbed the micro-glasses, then knelt down over Toddlandia, looking for signs of life.

The slipper they slept on, margarine tub they swam

in, and playground they played in were each empty. *Maybe they were all stuffing themselves on Mount Gym Clothes?* Wait a minute! Mount Gym Clothes was missing too!

Oh, yeah. That one was on me. I felt a little pang of guilt as I realized I'd forgotten to bring my gym clothes home this week to feed them.

Still, the Toddlians had to be around somewhere. I'd just talked to Lewis and Persephone only a few minutes ago.

Out in the living room, Max was slaughtering a C major scale, which was one of the last things Mom taught new kids on their first lesson. She must have had all she could stand and was cutting it extra short.

Where were they?

I flopped on my stomach and eyeballed every inch of Toddlandia. There was a light coming from the meeting hut, but I couldn't tell who was in there. Now that I was closer I understood why they hadn't heard me. The Toddlians were too busy yelling at each other. I'd never heard them fight before . . . what was going on? I shook my head. No time to worry about that now.

"All of you, come out here now!" I said, louder. I was sure Max wouldn't hear me over his meaty fingers banging out wrong notes.

The Toddlians started spilling out of the hut and

assembling on the pink bed slipper. "Wait, what happened, Herman?" I asked the limping Toddlian being helped along by Lewis and Persephone.

"I will explain, Your Greatness," he replied. "Pitiful sight that I am."

The piano went silent. "Oh, well . . . Get into this box right now!" I commanded.

"Why in tarnation should we?" Persephone huffed.

"Don't have time to explain! Just trust me! Hurry!" Some of the Toddlians on the slipper began to slowly creep toward the box. "No time for that!" I muttered, picking up the slipper, screaming Toddlians and all, and setting it in the box. The Toddlians were calling on me to be merciful, but I'd have to explain later that I was acting for their own safety.

Now, where to hide them? The bottom drawer of my dresser was partway open. I pulled it out, scooted aside some socks and underwear, and shut the Toddlians inside at the same second someone pounded on the door.

"Who is it?" I asked innocently. "I'm trying to take a nap in here, if you don't mind."

I heard Mom sigh. "Don't be ridiculous, Todd. Open the door; you have company."

I shoved the micro-glasses into my desk drawer and cracked the door a bit. Max pushed it the rest of the way open. He was grinning so hard I expected his face to split in half. There was a bunch of black Oreo shrapnel between his teeth. Mom gave all students cookies after their lesson, no matter how bad they'd sounded.

"Hey, Todd," Max said casually, walking in and plopping onto the end of my bed. "Wanna play?"

My guts twisted. "Actually, Max, I'm not feeling too good. My stomach hurts, so I think I'm just gonna snag some Zs, if you don't mind."

Mom came from behind Max and felt my forehead with the back of her hand. "Hmmm. No fever, so you're probably not contagious. You want me to bring you some Pepto-Bismol?"

"Yuck! I mean, um, no thanks, I'd probably just puke it up."

"Well, you can take it easy on your bed, and Max here can keep you company. Is that okay, Max?"

"Sure, Mrs. B," he schmoozed. "Thanks again for the lesson."

Mom smiled. "You're welcome. Good first effort, Max. You've got . . . very strong fingers." She left us alone, shutting the door behind her.

Max cracked his fingers one at a time as he backed me against the dresser. "Let's not make this more painful than it needs to be . . . for *you*, anyway." He swirled his head around like a hawk hunting prey. "Where are they?"

"Who?" I squeaked, pressing my foot firmly against the bottom drawer.

Max crossed his arms and glowered. "Don't play

games with me, Buttrock. Hand 'em over nice and easy."
He held his palm out.

I stalled. "The Toddlians aren't here."

His nostrils flared, which meant I was seconds from
annihilation. "Oh, they're here."

"No, seriously, I released them into the wild, so
they could be with nature and other bug-type creatures.
We drove them out into the woods last night and let
them go." I was in this deep, so I decided to pour on the
drama. I let out a deep, shuddery breath. "Almost broke
my heart, I tell ya. But it's what they wanted."

Max cocked his head and studied me from under his
unibrow. He wasn't buying it. "If they're gone, what's all
that?" He jerked his head toward Toddlandia.

Ugh. Why hadn't I shut the door? Without another
word, Max marched over to the closet and went full
Godzilla: wrecking the playground, dumping the water-
ing hole, slapping the sock (which the Toddlians didn't
use much anymore, not that he'd know that) against the
carpet . . .

"I told you, they aren't here," I said, holding my posi-
tion against the dresser.

Max ignored me and crossed to my desk. He tossed
baseball cards into the air, then used his arm like a bull-
dozer to sweep everything else off, sending my rubber-
band ball, my mug full of pens, and my newest *Dragon
Sensei* DVD toppling to the ground.

"You know," he seethed, rifling through the markers in my desk drawer, "I've thought long and hard about selling your little buggy-wuggies to science or some reality TV producer." He reached up onto the shelf that held all my *Dragon Sensei* drawings, flinging them to the floor. "But then I thought to myself, 'Max, why waste your time? Those little insects are bad luck. It'd probably just blow up in your face, like at the fair.'" In his hand was my best Saki drawing, the one where it looked like she was hurling a screaming Boom Shroom right off the page. I'd been seriously thinking about giving the picture to Charity when we role-played together—I mean, if she liked it.

Max shook the drawing at me. "But then I thought, wouldn't it be even sweeter to avenge myself on their teeny-weeny bodies—after they help me get an A on my science project, of course? Really pay them back for the pain they put me through?" My stomach flipped as he ripped the picture slowly in half from top to bottom. "Nobody makes a fool out of Max Loving."

I had to get him out of the room somehow.

My bed was his next assault. He shook the covers and then stuck his head under the bed. "Come here, buggy-wuggies," he cooed. "It's cold under here. Uncle Maxie wants to warm you up with a nice hot bonfire." He stood and said, all nonchalant, "I bought a blowtorch last week with my birthday money. Did you know that?"

I thought I'd hurl for real then, which, if I made enough noise, might at least get Mom back in the room.

But before I could toss my tots, Max shoved me out of the way and attacked the dresser, yanking open the top drawer and rummaging through my T-shirts.

"Max! Can't we talk about this?" I pleaded as he bent down to grab the bottom drawer handle. "Let me get you some more Oreos and—"

Mom popped her head in then, looking confused. "What's that? Max, are you looking for cookies? I'll have to send some home with you." She scoped out my floor. Her eyes rolled back, and I expected her head to spin. "Todd—" She glanced at Max. "We'll discuss your room in a minute. Max, your brother's here to take you home."

Max stood, frowning. The second Mom trotted off to collect the cookies, he lunged for me. "I could wring your neck like a chicken," he snarled, proving it by putting me in a death grip.

"You're killing me," I wheezed.

"Naw. You're not worth it." His claws opened, and I collapsed, gasping for air. "But I swear I will find those critters. If not today, tomorrow. And once I've showed 'em to Mr. Katcher and gotten my A . . . I'm gonna turn up the heat!"

The car horn blared a couple of times, cutting off Max's evil cackle. "All right!" Max breathed through clenched teeth. "I'm coming!" He stomped to the door, then turned and pointed at me. "I'll be back, Buttrock.

And I'm going to barbecue your little buggies over an open flame! That's a promise."

As soon as I heard the car squeal away, I shut the door to my room and pulled the Toddlians out of their hiding spot. I set the shoebox on the dresser. They were, of course, freaking out, screaming, "GREAT TODD, SAVE US!" and a bunch of other stuff I couldn't understand.

"I'm working on it, okay!" I rasped. I wondered if Max had bruised my windpipe. It sure felt like it. But I didn't have time to worry about that now. I needed a safe place to keep the Toddlians. Somewhere Max couldn't just barge into.

Lucy's house! Lucy had always wanted to share them with me anyway. I leaned my face down next to the box. That hushed them. "OK, guys, you have to go on a little retreat to Lucy's. Like, right now."

Lewis spoke up. "Oh, Great Todd live forever—"

"Make it quick!" I said. "We have to hurry!"

"Sorry," he said meekly. "What is a 'retreat'?"

"It's kinda like a vacation where you go and kick back. You don't do anything but . . . think and stuff." I grabbed the lid and started to cover them.

But Lewis wasn't finished. "Great Todd!" he squeaked in a higher voice than usual. "Forgive me, but do you mean to say that a retreat is a place to reflect . . . erm, that is, to consider the things that one might have done wrong?"

"Exactly. No more questions—gotta go!"

Lewis whimpered, and I threw on the micro-glasses and stuck my head into the box for an up-close look at the little dude. He looked kinda pasty. Weird. But I didn't have time to worry about that right now.

I took off the glasses, put the shoebox under my arm, and peeked in at Mom, who was busy with another student. I scribbled a note for her on the message board in the kitchen, then sneaked out the front door and hustled across the street to Lucy's house.

"Why, Todd!" sang Mrs. Pedoto as she opened the door. She had a wooden spoon in her hand and a big brown ceramic mixing bowl on her hip. "It's so good to see you!" she said, waving the spoon around as she talked. "Now you just come inside and tell me all about your day while I whip up this vegan and sugar-free baklava. You'll have to taste it!"

I had no idea what baklava was, but I'd tried her cardboard-flavored sugar-free concoctions before and had definitely learned my lesson. "Umm, I'd love to," I lied, "but I really need to ask Lucy's advice about my science homework."

Mrs. Pedoto's voice trailed after me as I hurried down the hall. "You do that. I'm sure she'll be thrilled to see you!"

I knocked on Lucy's bedroom door and said, "Lucy?"

Lucy threw the door open. Her dark eyes sparkled as she said, "Todd! I'm so glad you're here! You're just in time. My male seahorse is about to give birth. See?"

I followed her to the tank on her dresser. "Uh, did you say the *male* was giving birth?"

"Mm-hmm, see?" She started twisting the end of one black braid nervously. "His respirations are speeding up, and his color is changing from gray to a yellowish-tan . . . Breathe, Neptune! Don't lose focus," she crooned. "Here they come!"

Countless minuscule seahorses shot out of the hole in Neptune's belly as he jerked his tail upward. I felt myself gag, but at the same time, I couldn't look away. The seahorse gave one more convulsion and dropped, exhausted, to the bottom of the tank.

Lucy congratulated the new family with some frozen shrimp and then turned to me. "Well, next to discovering the Toddlians, that's the coolest thing I've ever witnessed." She cocked her head and stared at me. "Are you sick, Todd? Your voice is kind of hoarse." Lucy glanced back at the tank. "Oh, speaking of horses, here comes another one! You'll have to help me name them all."

"Yeah, sure." I held out the box of Toddlians to her. "Errrm . . . I brought you something. I kind of need a favor."

Lucy gave me a strange smile and blinked a couple of times. She pulled the lid off the box, and some of the Toddlians cheered. "Oh, hello!" she said. "I've missed you guys!"

"We've sure as shootin' missed you!" a voice hollered back from the box. *Persephone.*

"Miss Lucy!" Herman's voice piped up, just as delighted as Persephone. "In the words of Shakespeare: 'All days are nights to see till I see thee, And nights bright days when dreams do show thee to me.' "

I rolled my eyes. But Lucy smiled down and thanked them before glancing up at me with concern. "Wait, Todd, is everything okay? What kind of favor do you need?"

I didn't want to worry Lucy, so I kept things vague. "I just need you to watch them for a while until I get some things worked out."

She tilted her head and looked at me curiously. "Right . . . Well, of course, Todd. That's what friends are for."

Friends. A couple of weeks ago I never would have considered Lucy a *friend,* but now I was glad I did.

Mrs. Pedoto knocked twice on the door and then pushed it open. Lucy hid the shoebox behind her back. "Todd, your mom called and said it's time to come home for dinner. But I told her you'd be welcome to eat with us . . ."

"Oh, I wish I could," I fibbed. Mrs. Pedoto's cardboard-tasting baked goods were mouthwatering treats compared to her meals. "But . . ." I threw in a sniffle to pluck the heartstrings. "It's just my Dad's been pulling double shifts this week, and I've hardly gotten to see him."

Mrs. Pedoto nodded, her red ponytail bouncing. "I totally understand. Family time is precious." She blew a kiss to Lucy, who blushed. "Are you getting a cold,

Todd? I picked up some lemon chamomile herb drops this afternoon at the Health Hub. Let me send some home with you." With that she trotted off.

When I turned around, Lucy was slowly lifting the slipper out of the shoebox and placing it on the bed. I took a deep breath. Weird as it made me feel to leave the Toddlians with someone else, I knew Lucy would take good care of them. I needed some time to figure out how to handle Max . . . *And,* I realized, *if the Toddlians aren't in my room, maybe I can have Charity over to role-play!*

"Thanks for trusting me with the Toddlians," Lucy said.

"Of course. You've helped save them more than once, remember?"

Before I could say anything else, some of the Toddlians started chanting, "LU-CY, LU-CY, LU-CY!"

Their chanting gave me a weird feeling in my chest. "Well . . . I guess you guys will be okay, then, uh, without me," I said to Lucy, forcing a quick smile. "Um . . . I should go."

"Todd—" Lucy began, but I was already at her bedroom door. I pretended not to hear her as I rushed down the hallway, out her front door, and into the cool, clear night.

CHAPTER 6
HERMAN

Lucy set our sleeping quarters onto her carpet and said, "I have to appease my parents by making a dinner appearance, but I'll be back as soon as I can."

The moment she shut the door, I called a conference. We had much to discuss. Earlier that day, when Persephone had told us about Todd's lacking response to Lewis's concerns, many of my people were alarmed.

"What shall we do, Mayor Herman?" Gerald the Elder had asked as the others chattered amongst themselves. "Without Todd, we have no food source, no guidance . . ."

In response, I'd limped to the border of Toddlandia and pointed toward the shriveled Thing. "I suggest we send a party of our bravest Toddlians to examine the Red Thing for a message. This morning, we were distracted by the . . . worm. But perhaps, in our haste to escape, we missed the greater meaning."

There was a murmur of agreement. Persephone volunteered to lead the posse as long as we went by cricketback.

But our fact-finding mission was, once again, doomed. When we'd reached what was left of the Red Thing, Persephone clambered up to the hole, the pistol that she'd fashioned out of a paper clip drawn and ready. But soon she'd shouted down, "It's skedaddled! No sign of it!"

First the Toddlian posse cheered. "Maybe this is a sign that Todd has forgiven us!" Lewis called out. Persephone began working her way down the wrinkled skin when I heard a low rumble that changed into an overpowering *BUZZZZZ.*

The sound was loud enough to shake the ground. It brought about a fear in me that I had not felt since that terrible Max Loving attempted to teach me a high-wire act.

"GERONIMO!" Persephone screamed, hurling herself into the Fiber Forest. She hit hard and rolled over as the rest of us fled.

"AAAUUUGGGHHH!" cried the crowd. The crickets had run off in the confusion, and somehow we all managed to get home to Toddlandia before the source of the horrible noise could show itself.

With a heavy heart, I led my people to the big round structure we'd just finished a week before—our Meeting Hut—and moved to the lectern, one of Todd's Lego blocks.

"My fellow Toddlandians," I'd said, "today we have reached a crisis the likes of which our people have never known. Lewis, you know our god better than anyone here. What is your inner wisdom, my friend?"

Lewis kept his head down and said softly, "I feel our loyalty is being tested. Perhaps we need to try harder to please Todd."

I nodded slowly. "Yes, perhaps we should endeavor to more effectively please him or—" I understood Lewis's devotion, but I felt I had to share my truth as well. "Or perhaps it's time we found ourselves another god."

Back in the present I climbed a stack of scientific journals beside Lucy's desk, making a mental note to read through them if time allowed, and instructed my fellow Toddlians to gather upon Lucy's close-cropped forest of fibers. "Citizens of Toddlandia! I think we can all agree after recent events that Great Todd is angry with us. I think perhaps Todd has left us with Lucy because he has . . . he has grown tired of us."

"You mean forsaken us?" Gerald the Elder asked in horror.

The people began to wail, and there were cries of woe: "What's to be done?" "Who will save us?" "We're DOOOOOMED!"

I raised my hands until everyone settled. I called to mind the words I had read in *Encyclopedia Britannica*, volume *R*, during the time of our captivity under Max. "Let us not panic. In the words of that noble lady, Eleanor Roosevelt: 'You gain strength, courage, and confidence by every experience in which you really stop to look fear in the face. You must do the thing you think you cannot do.' Now is not the time for fear but for *action*. Perhaps, as Lewis says, we owe it to ourselves to try to get back into Todd's good graces and regain his favor, before taking more . . . dramatic actions." I paused, swallowing hard. "Any suggestions?"

Martin, a particularly lively youth, waved his arm wildly until I acknowledged him. "We could all dress up like characters from *Dragon Sensei*! I hereby volunteer to play Mongee-Poo." He began to "HOO-HOO" and "HI-YAH!" while cavorting about recklessly. Some of the elders objected to the indignity of such a scheme, much to Martin's disappointment.

One of our maternal people made a more rational plan. "We could make him one of those Nitro Chicken Burgers like they serve at Cluck 'N' Chuck. He practically licks the screen when one of those commercials comes on."

Lewis's face lit up. "I can sing the jingle and do the chicken dance!" He bent his elbows and flapped about madly, singing, *"Are ya tired of salad? Are ya sick of soup? Get your hungry on! Come down to our coop!"* Several of the younger Toddlians joined in, clucking and mooing so I could not hear myself think. Finally Persephone whistled, stopping the ruckus.

It was not long before we realized we could not manage the actual capture and killing of a chicken. Despite Persephone's valiant offers to do the "fowl" deed, we had no idea where to find such a bird, dead or alive.

Before we had formed any feasible plan, Lucy returned to her bedroom and knelt down beside us, donning her magnification spectacles.

"How was your dinner?" I inquired.

"Uh . . . nutritious," she replied. "Stir-fried shitake and baby bok choy."

"Oh, dear," I said. "I am not familiar with the race of bok choy, but eating any kind of infant is firmly against my principles."

Lucy giggled. "Baby bok choy is tender Chinese cabbage, and shitake is a kind of mushroom. Fungus is full of folic acid, an essential vitamin at my time of life. I'm still a little hungry, though."

"No wonder! Poor Lucy, having to eat such things! It must be a terrible trial to be human. I am sorry you will be hungry this evening." It was a sensation that had become all too familiar.

"Don't feel too sorry for me," Lucy said with a wink. We all gasped as she reached into her lab coat pocket and pulled out . . . was that a *Red Thing*? Yes, it had the same beautiful round shape, smooth red skin, and leafy stem! We knew too well that soon the skin would shrivel and curl, the stem grow fuzzy, the leaf wither, and the white flesh grow brown and slimy. Did Lucy realize her danger? Did she know that changeable Thing harbored horrible beasts?

Lucy tossed it in the air, caught it, and crossed to her dresser. She seemed completely unafraid. Was this another sign? Had Todd given the Red Thing to her?

We did not wait to see what would become of the treacherous object; we ran as one screaming mass into the furthermost corner of the Slipper to hide. *"Another message!" "Watch out for the Worm!" "What will become of us?"* wailed the Toddlians.

Then Lewis implored, "Someone, please! Go see what she does with it!"

My people stood cowering in the darkest part of the Slipper. Not even brave Persephone spoke up. "I will go," I said finally. "As the poet Robert Frost put it: 'Freedom lies in being bold.'"

"You ain't facin' that Thing alone!" Persephone cried, rallying to my side.

Lewis joined her. "I wish to be free as well . . . I

think." He slung my arm over his shoulder. I was glad of it; my injured ankle was throbbing incessantly.

Lucy's face was hovering over us as we emerged. "Hey! Where'd you guys go?"

We fixed our astonished eyes on Lucy. She was actually *eating* the Red Thing! "Is that Thing . . . *food*?" I ventured to ask.

"Of course," Lucy said around a bite. Juice dribbled down her chin, and she wiped it away with the back of her hand. "Would you like to try it?" She pushed the Thing in our direction, and we stumbled backward. Even brave Persephone let out a little scream.

"It won't hurt you," Lucy promised. "It's merely *Malus domestica*, commonly known as an apple. This variety is a Red Delicious, although I prefer Gala. Susan— that's my mom—never buys them; she's under the common misconception that the darker the skin, the more nutritional the content."

Lucy tossed the core of the apple into a Refuse Dome, and our trio exhaled in unison. "Told ya it weren't nothin' to worry about," Persephone boasted.

"That may be," I answered. "But it still does not solve our problems."

Lewis sighed and slumped onto the floor.

"What's the matter with him?" Lucy asked. "What's the matter with all of you? Pardon my saying so, but you all seem pretty bummed, yanno?"

"Translation, please," I said.

Lucy rested her chin on her fist. "Bummed, depressed, downcast . . ."

"Ah—" I began, but I did not want to betray our frustrations with Todd to Lucy. Not until all hope was lost.

Persephone had no such scruples. "Yer darn tootin' we're bums or whatever ya call it. That fool Todd—"

"—didn't take time to feed us before we left," I interrupted.

"Really?" Lucy said, raising her eyebrows. "I wonder why? Hmm . . . So you're hungry?" Lucy jumped up and scanned her room. "Let's see . . ." She crossed back to the dresser and picked up various bottles. "Hmm. Turtle Tidbits . . . No, that's too low in protein, plus it contains algae, which might turn your stomachs sour."

My stomach was turning already.

She picked up another bottle. "Tarantula Treats . . . No, that's mostly dead crickets. Hey! How about mealworms? Those are full of protein, and I've got a tub of little live ones in the fridge!"

Lucy dashed out of her room and in no time was back with a white carton. She popped the lid off and dangled a wriggling brown-striped worm over us.

Lewis whimpered, and I was about to protest when Persephone whipped out her paper-clip pistol. "We ain't eatin' no creepy crawlies, Miss Lucy. No offense, but iffin one of those mealy things comes near me, I'll blow it clean into tomorrow."

Lucy smiled a little and put the worms away. She

let out a long breath and glanced around her room once more. "If only Todd had thought to bring along some of his dirty laundry. Mine's all clean . . ." Her eyes rested on her bed. "Except for this!" She shook the covering off her pillow and held it up for us to examine. Upon a white background was printed a series of colorful squares she called a "periodic table."

"I haven't washed it in five days, so there should be approximately" — she shut her eyes and muttered a string of enormous numbers — "approximately three hundred thousand dead skin cells for you to feast upon. You can indulge and learn about chemistry at the same time! Will that do?" she asked.

Ah, a decent meal at last! I bowed to her. "On behalf of the Toddlians, we are most truly grateful for your gift of delicious dirt!"

Lucy nodded and crossed her arms. "Well, go ahead. Taste it!"

We obeyed. "Mmmm," Lewis and I hummed as we chewed. Compared to the crisp, salty goodness of Todd dirt, Lucy's dirt was bland and rather sticky. But we grinned and "mmmm"ed anyway. Beggars could not be choosy chewers.

"So what do you think?" Lucy asked expectantly. "Is it as good as Todd's? Be completely honest, now."

Lewis and I looked at each other. "Ahem," I said. "Well, while there is nothing wrong with your wonderful dirt, we were created from Todd, so naturally his dirt suits our palate better."

"Horse nuggets!" Persephone huffed. She grabbed a handful of dirt from the pillowcase and stuffed it into her mouth, wincing slightly. "This is . . . the *best-tastin'* grub I ever ate. And so healthy! I can barely swaller down Todd dirt; that nasty nacho cheese aftertaste burns the belly. She*weeee!*"

Lewis explained the mystery of the Red Thing (which we now knew was once an edible apple) to our people as Lucy spread out her pillowcase so everyone could eat their fill. But that still didn't account for the worm creature or the deafening droning noise. I still believed it might be a sign that Todd was preparing to abandon us.

Unfortunately, most of our friends agreed with Lewis and me about the food; Lucy's leavings were less appetizing than Todd's, no matter how many times Persephone shoved our arms and said, "Mmm, mmm! Ain't that the tastiest grub you ever did eat?"

After everyone had eaten all they could stand, Lucy looked us all over and made her observation. "You guys seemed stressed out. What's really going on? Why do you look so worried?"

Lewis glanced at me, and I nodded. He took a deep breath and asked, "How would one know when their god has . . . forsaken them?"

We all studied Lucy, who was obviously startled.

She mused for a moment and then said quite seriously, "Maybe Todd's just got something on his mind. Knowing him, that's probably the case. After all, if he didn't care about you, he wouldn't have brought you to me, now would he?" Lucy didn't look as sure as she sounded.

"Could he be testing us?" I suggested.

She furrowed her brow and then nodded. "Well . . . almost all of the world's religions have a point in their mythologies where the 'god' has tested the devotion of its followers."

"Oooo," we chorused. I knew we had been right to appeal to Lucy's higher wisdom.

"Um, I'm not sure what Todd is doing, but let's break this down." Lucy wheeled her whiteboard over and uncapped a blue marker. She shoved her magnification spectacles up onto her forehead and wrote "history of comparative religions" across the top. Below that, she scribbled "buddhism," "roman mythology," "judaism," "christianity," "hinduism," "islam," and "taoism."

Jasper the youth regarded the board skeptically. "Do any of these gods try to devour their subjects with a huge terrifying worm?" he asked.

Lucy coughed. "Um. Well, no. But, for comparison, Kali, the Hindu goddess of destruction, evil, and death, is so fearsome she wears skulls around her neck."

"Just like Saki!" Lewis exclaimed.

"The *Dragon Sensei* salamander princess? Mm-hmm.

When Kali's angry with the activities of people, she wreaks all kinds of havoc."

Lewis spoke again. "Do you have any stories of angry gods punishing their people for doing something wrong, but then restoring them to their former place of favor . . . and *friendship*?"

Lucy looked thoughtful. "Well, sure. Several cultures and religions share some form of flood account. But in these instances it's generally the 'good' people who are rescued, and everyone else is wiped out . . . For instance, the Hopi tribe have a tale of a great flood in which a Spider Grandmother sealed righteous people inside of boats made from reeds, and they sailed away safely to what was known as the Fourth World."

"Oooo," we replied, although none of us was very keen on the idea of assistance from elderly arachnids. Still, there was something intriguing about the tale.

"What are some other flood accounts?" I inquired.

"Well, Judaism and Christianity share the story of a creator so fed up with the behavior of humanity that he warned people to change their ways. When they remained evil, he told a good man named Noah to build an enormous boat, called an ark, and gather two of every beast and bird. When they were all safe inside, he sent a deluge of massive proportions and opened the fountains of the deep, flooding the entire planet. He basically started over."

My *mind* was being flooded. I needed to hear that one again. "Could you repeat that last bit, about the ark? It would have to be enormous!"

Lucy nodded. "Bible scholars speculate that it was taller than a three-story building and as long and as wide as a football field."

I was speechless.

"Oh, and I forgot to mention that when God gave Noah instructions to build his floating zoo, it had never rained before. So it really *was* a test of Noah's faith and devotion.

"Now . . . moving on to Buddhism. What really attracts me to the teachings of the Buddha is the emphasis that wealth does not guarantee happiness. In our materialistic society—"

"Wait!" I was not ready to move on. "How did Noah get all of those animals on the ark? Did he have to capture them, or were they divinely drawn to him?"

Lucy tapped the marker against her temple. "Not sure. It doesn't really matter if the end result was the same, does it? Now, the Buddha—"

"So did all of the earth's inhabitants have a warning that the flood was coming? Did only Noah survive by entering the boat?"

Lucy sighed. "According to the Old Testament there were actually eight onboard the ark: Noah, his wife, their three sons, and their wives. Now, let's look at the teachings of—"

"What's a 'testament'?" Marty wanted to know.

Lucy looked as if she was beginning to lose patience. "It's part of the Bible, okay? There's an old one and a new one. Can we move on now?"

There was a gentle knock at the door, and Lucy's maternal person peeped in. "Are you on the phone, Lu? To whom are you talking?"

"Myself," Lucy said. "Just writing out some calculus proofs to help me relax before going to bed—like counting sheep?"

Susan chuckled. "Clever girl. Well, you might want to turn off your light. It's getting late, and every hour before midnight—"

"Is worth two after," Lucy finished. "See you in the morning."

"Pleasant REM sleep!" Susan sang as she clicked the door closed.

Lucy knelt down by us and stifled a yawn. "Why don't we call it a night, guys? There's plenty of time to continue our discussion of divinity tomorrow."

She went to her closet and brought back a large, rectangular white box. Opening it, she pulled a lavender sweater out from under pink tissue paper and then spread the sweater at the foot of her bed. "This sweater is made of angora. It was my grandmother's—she actually knitted the fur from her very own rabbit! I mean, from the fur it shed; she didn't hurt her rabbit or anything. It's the softest thing I own, and will make a warm, snuggly bed," Lucy explained with a tender smile. "I can't wash it, so it's probably covered in edible 'Lucy dirt.'"

I was already feeling warm from the kindness of Lucy, which was so different from the treatment of our god lately. The softest thing Todd had ever given us was the Slipper—and that seemed so very long ago.

Once nuzzled into our warm bed, we were quite still . . . except for an occasional "Achoo!" Apparently some of us were allergic to angora. We waited quietly until we heard Lucy's snores. We didn't have to wait long.

"What if he never takes us back?" worried Cynthia, a tiny Toddlian.

"I miss Todd!" another young Toddlian named Milly cried.

"Hush now, and close your eye-peeps," I assured them with a pat on the head. "All will be well, I promise."

But was it a promise I could keep?

"Suppose he takes us back," whispered an Old One, "but serves us an even worse punishment than the Red Thing? Remember how it caused you to injure your ankle? What if it had been little Milly or Cynthia instead of you?"

Gerald agreed. "How many more of us must suffer harm? I am not certain how much more persecution our people can endure."

Persephone hopped up and declared, "Y'all are makin' a mudslide outta a cowpie."

Lewis shook his head. "What?"

"Look, Herman got it right after we got away from that buzzin' varmint," she said. "We need us a new god." Several of the Toddlians cheered, waking the sleeping wee ones. Persephone pointed at Lucy's uncovered foot. "Yer answer's right in front of ya. We can hunker down right here in her lab and never have to fret over food again."

"But I'm *starving*!" Lewis moaned, and others agreed. "Lucy dirt has no substance or flavor; it's not even filling!"

Chester's crackly voice rose above the rest. "If Lucy becomes our new god, can we at least sneak her some junk food? I need Oreo dirt! Like yesterday!"

"OR-E-OS!" someone chanted. It caught like a wildfire. "OR-E-OS! OR-E-OS!"

As Persephone quieted the crowd, I closed my eyes and meditated on what Lucy had said about Noah. *Could we start over as a civilization in a new world?* I wondered. *How long would it take us to build a watertight craft that could hold us all and have enough room for two of every creature?*

"If you will all please be still and listen for a minute," I implored. "An idea has come to me . . ."

CHAPTER 7

The next day after school, Duddy and I suited up for swim team tryouts. The school supplied swim caps and goggles, but we had to come up with our own trunks. At least my blue-and-red Superman trunks still fit. Duddy's bright yellow trunks looked about two sizes too small and were covered in sunglasses-wearing starfish.

I tugged at my trunks as we walked out of the locker room. "I hope the Toddlians are okay," I muttered. "I usually try to give them a snack after school. I mean, when I remember."

"They're fine," said Duddy, pulling out a nose clip and shoving it onto his nostrils. "Lucy will dake good care of dem."

I nodded, knowing he was right. Still, I'd feel better with the Toddlians back under my own roof.

Duddy had invited his *Dragon Sensei* role-playing buddies, Ike and Wendell, to be our cheering section. He wanted to include Ernie, he explained, but figured it might have been awkward, with Ernie just being kicked off the team and all. Ike and Wendell were standing in the bleachers as we came out of the changing room, giving us the three-fingered Saki Salute. "HOO-YA HI-YA—" Wendell began.

"KEEP THAT RACKET DOWN!" A voice suddenly boomed from the small office behind the bleachers, and I turned to see a guy—he must have been six feet tall, made out of granite, with a shaved head—appear in the doorway, shaking his fist at Wendell.

Wendell looked like he was about to pee himself. "S-so s-sorry, Coach Tomlin," he said, quickly sitting down. "Didn't—er—didn't mean to—"

"Oh, you d-didn't, eh?" the Granite Man yelled back. "It's bad enough this flower show of a sport takes place right outside my office. At least keep it down!" He walked back into his office and slammed the door behind him, loud enough to make the kids across the pool jump.

Duddy turned to me with wide eyes. "Do you know who dat is?" he asked.

"Mr. Clean's very angry brother?" I joked.

But Duddy shook his head solemnly. "Dat's Coach Domlin. Da eighth grade gym coach. Dey call 'im 'Derrifying Coach Domlin.' Dere's a rumor he drew a garbage can ad a kid one dime."

I shrugged, looking back at the closed office door. "Wouldn't surprise me. Well, I guess we'd better hope we're on the WAVES by eighth grade, to avoid that guy."

Duddy nodded. "I hope Wendell's all right." He pointed to the crowd of kids milling about in bathing suits by the deep end. "Look, dere dey are! Dude! Dat's a wot of kids for dree spots."

"Yeah," I said, clutching my towel tight. "Must be at least forty of them. Do we even have a shot?"

Duddy shoved his goggles onto his forehead and stared at me solemnly. "Wemember why we're doing dis, Todd." He jerked his head toward the deep end. "Da same weason all dose udder kids are here: da getting-out-of-gym card is just doo good do pass up. And dey've probably heard about Madame P's crêpes."

I frowned at him. "Dud, do you have to wear that nose thing? You realize you sound kinda like Ernie, right?"

Duddy nodded solemnly. "Widdoud da clip, I jus' *suck in* wadder. Like a bacuum. I dink dere's someding wrong wif my nose."

Fair enough. Just then Charity emerged from the girls' dressing room, wearing a black and pink polka-dot suit. She hadn't put her cap on yet, and her hair covered her shoulders like a shiny cape. I certainly wasn't the only guy with my eyes glued to her, yet by some miracle, it was me she turned to and winked at. *Me.*

I don't know how long I stood there, boiling in my own embarrassment. Charity walked by with a soft "Hi, Todd." I followed her tropical scent across the damp cement to where Duddy and the other kids were lining up.

The delicious tingle dulled enough for me to snap back to reality. *No way* was I going to lose face in front of Charity. I actually had a chance with her, and the second I hit the water I'd blow it. "Let me know how it goes," I whispered to Duddy, yanking off my goggles. "I just remembered I'm supposed to babysit Daisy while Mom has a lesson."

I'd already made it to the four-foot mark when Duddy caught me by the arm, panting through his mouth since his nose was blocked. "*Huhhhh. Huhhhh.* Dodd, dere's no way you're backing out on me now. Just dink! *We can be fwee fwom gym class! Fwom swirlies! Fwom wedgies! Fwom Ma—*" Duddy went whiter than he already was. I followed his gaze and saw why.

Max had just strutted out of the boys' dressing room. In a black Speedo. He puffed out his furry gorilla chest and tried to shove his bushy black hair under the silver WAVES swim cap. He snapped on his goggles and headed right toward us.

I looked at Duddy and raised my eyebrows. He

nodded. Without further discussion, we disobeyed the laminated ABSOLUTELY NO RUNNING! signs that hung all around the pool and beat it to the back of the line.

Stupid extracurriculars! How was I supposed to keep the Toddlians safe when Max seemed to be following me wherever I went?

"Dis is so not good," Duddy said. I'd already filled him in about Mom's new piano student and how he'd nearly killed me and the Toddlians last night.

"Understatement of the century," I whispered, trying to crouch down and blend in with all the other skinny, silver-domed boys.

Duddy did the same, whimpering, "What if we bof make da deam, bud so does *he*?"

I peeked behind me and saw Max standing just one kid away. "We will quit like sane people and go buy our own flippin' crêpes," I hissed.

"There's Madame Dauphinee," Duddy said, nodding toward the low board.

A mom-aged woman in a silver skirted bathing suit, with poofy black hair twisted up in a bun, waddled to the end of the board and sat on it sideways. *"Bonjour!"* she called to us, putting on the cat-eye glasses that dangled from a chain around her neck. "Welcome to the Wakefield WAVES swim team tryouts." She pulled a clipboard out from under her arm. "WAVES stands for Water Athletes Victorious Every Swim, and in this club we celebrate every effort, win or lose!"

Duddy leaned toward me, adjusting his schnoz blocker. "Dold you she was awesome!"

"Let's see now," Madame Dauphinee said, scanning the clipboard. "Three spots, one boy and two girls, taken from forty-one potential team members. Hmmm." She tapped her pen against her cheek for a moment, then hopped up and pointed to a tall, athletic girl. "Maya is the captain of the WAVES, and she will divide you into seven groups of five and one group of six."

While Maya counted us off, Madame Dauphinee climbed down from the diving board, shrugged off her fluffy white robe, and unwound her bun into an impossibly long braid. We got into our groups, and then she picked up the whistle around her neck and gave a shrill blast, planting her hands on her hips. "Two laps, any stroke of your choice. Fastest boy and two girls will replace our fallen WAVES warriors. Maya, will you demonstrate?"

Maya nodded at Madame Dauphinee, grabbed a red rubber swim cap that read CAPTAIN from the bleachers and pulled it tightly over her hair, then bounded into the air and dove under the water. When she surfaced, she sliced through the pool like a meteor, churning up a foamy tail behind her.

"Whoa," Duddy breathed.

After two laps, she popped back onto the side of the pool, water pouring off her athletic black suit, and raised her arms in a victory sign. Madame Dauphinee smiled at her and clapped, then turned to us. "Voilà! See how easy? Now it's your turn!"

"Dat didn't look doo easy," Duddy muttered, tapping his plug.

I glanced at him in alarm. "Dud, are you sure you want to do this?"

Duddy had a faraway look in his eyes, but after a few seconds he gave me a determined look. "Yeah, I'm sure. Led's do dis!"

He held out his hand for a fist bump, and I grinned and gave it to him.

I turned around to find Maya picking two kids per heat to keep time. Duddy and I were in the last heat. With another shrill whistle, the first group dove into the water, and tryouts began.

I pushed to the front of the crowd so I could get a better view. Charity was one of the first swimmers. She took a deep breath, stretched her arms, and shook her legs. Madame Dauphinee called, "On your mark!" The whistle sounded, and Charity cut a graceful arc through the air before disappearing under the water without even making a splash. Her arms swung over her head and carved through the water; her back and legs rippled like a mermaid's tail.

Charity pushed off the wall and flipped around, butterflying toward me. When she sprung up for air, I had to blink—I could have sworn I was seeing the Lizard

Queen rising out of the Fernsopian pool in all her glory. Glistening drops of water scattered in slow motion as the queen plunged back below the surface.

"*Très bon!*" Madame Dauphinee said to Charity as she pulled herself out of the pool. "Congratulations! You won your heat!" Charity peeled her cap and goggles off, then shook out her hair, which fell right back into the gorgeous golden waterfall I was always daydreaming about.

I must have been staring like a complete goober, because Duddy elbowed me and said, "Shud your mouf, Dodd."

Charity wrapped up in her towel and walked over to me. "Good luck," she said, winking. I wanted to tell her she'd done an amazing job, but the words were stuck in my throat.

Max didn't have any such problems. As soon as she walked past him, he said, "Nice swimmin', sweetie." Charity lifted her lip like she smelled something bad and gave him an icy glare.

Duddy elbowed me again. "Did you see dat?!"

Yeah, terrific. One more reason for Max to obliterate me.

When Duddy and I stood to get into the pool for our heat, so did Max. I didn't like being so close to Max one bit, but I decided to just ignore him. He couldn't make me swim any worse, right? When it was our turn, I lined up on the blocks with the other swimmers. I had Max on my left and Duddy to my right. Ike and Wendell were HOO-HOOing and HI-YAHing so loud in the stands that Madame Dauphinee threatened to kick them out. Duddy shot me a shaky thumbs-up.

"You okay?" I asked him.

"Ob course!" he said, shoving his nose plug in a little farther. "J-jusd a little c-c-old."

"Get ready, Buttrock!" Max growled beside me. I looked straight ahead, trying to focus on the black lines at the bottom of the pool. What was I afraid of, anyway? It wasn't like he could hurt the Toddlians here. But I could still see him out of the corner of my eye as he pounded one fist into the other. "Hope you're not scared to drown, 'cause you're goin' *down.*"

My stomach did a somersault, and I tried to think of a way to switch lanes . . . or just get out of there. I could pass out . . . no, Max might pretend to do CPR and kill me for real.

Madame Dauphinee put us on our mark then, and I bent over and gripped the edge of the platform. When she gave the signal to go, I dove into the water and rocketed through it, hugging the right side of my lane. My heart pounded in my ears. I expected to feel Max's fist around my ankle any second.

I came up for my first stroke and looked under my arm. *What?* I'd left Max, and everybody else, in my wake. My feet turned into turbo-flippers, and I slashed the water with my arms, giving the name *freestyle* a whole new meaning. *Beat Max! Beat Max! Beat Max!* I thought with every stroke.

By the time I was halfway down the lane, I'd pulled way ahead. I broke rhythm and glanced back to see how Duddy was doing. Wait. *Where was Duddy?* He wasn't in his lane.

I stopped swimming and turned just in time to see Max reach out and push Duddy's head under water. Duddy let out a wail, but the sound was lost in all the splashing and cheering of the crowd. I didn't think anyone else had seen it. Duddy was just barely staying afloat to begin with, and Max's shove left him bobbing up and down like a buoy on a stormy lake. He drifted into my lane, trying to dog paddle, churning up the water, going in crazy circles . . . *going under!*

Does he seriously not know how to swim?

I swam toward him, not stopping to breathe. *DUD-DY! DUD-DY! DUD-DY!* my heart pounded.

When I got close, I dove down until I found him. Looping my arms around his chest, I kicked like crazy for the surface. I gasped for air the second we cleared the water, but Duddy didn't. Madame Dauphinee leaned down, and together we got him hoisted over the edge of the pool.

Duddy lay limp on the pukey green tile, and for a

sickening second I thought we'd been too late. Madame Dauphinee yanked his nose plug out and rolled him onto his side. He started coughing—spewing water. It looked like he'd drunk half the pool.

I leaned with my hands on my knees, not taking my eyes off my best friend. After a minute, Duddy sat up and gave me a wobbly smile. "Thanks for rescuing me, Todd."

"Don't mention it," I panted.

"What happened in there?" Madame Dauphinee asked Duddy. "Did you get a cramp?"

He shook his head, still dazed. "Can't swim, really."

She muttered some stuff in French and helped him stand. "Why did you try out then? Don't you know you could have drowned?"

Duddy shrugged. "I really like crêpes."

She smiled then. "May I suggest that it will be much safer if you just take French class? I make crêpes every other Friday."

Ike and Wendell ran up and started thumping me on the back and calling me things like "SharkTruese Jr." I could tell they were about to make a scene, so I wrapped Duddy's towel around his shoulders and said, "Madame Dauphinee, can Duddy go sit in the stands? I think he needs to rest."

She nodded, and we led him away. "Dudster," I said as we parked ourselves on the bottom bleacher, "don't you *ever* pull something like that again. Got it?"

"Got it." He grinned. "Anyway, pool water tastes like bleached pee. You're going to have to eat a lot of crêpes to get *that* taste out of your mouth."

In all the excitement with Duddy I'd forgotten about making the team. We still had to have the swim-offs, where the fastest swimmers from each round would race against each other. Max was showboating about having won the last heat, which had really been no contest since he'd been the only one who kept swimming once Duddy started to drown.

Madame Dauphinee cut Max off. "Nobody won the last heat because of . . . well, as I said, there are no losers among the Wakefield WAVES. To *try* is to be victorious!"

"So who makes it to the swim-offs?" Max demanded. "It's not like all of us from the last heat can go."

Amanda Phillips, an eighth grade honor student, raised her hand. "Madame Dauphinee, I was keeping time for the last heat, and Max's time was 28.46 seconds. That's pretty fast—faster than half the kids already competing in the swim-off."

Max grinned at Amanda, giving her a wink. She turned red.

Madame Dauphinee tapped her pen against her clipboard and stared at the ceiling. "I suppose, all things considered, the only fair thing to do is hold the swim-off as planned."

Max made a point of glaring at every winner of the other heats, except Charity. His meaning was clear.

Jordan McAfee's hand shot in the air. He'd won the second heat. "It's okay, Madame Dauphinee, Max's time was faster than mine. I-I don't feel up to a swim-off; I'm just exhausted."

The other winners agreed. Apparently staying alive was more important to them than making the team.

"So I guess we don't have to have a swim-off after all," Max announced, nodding at Jordan and the other winners with a big smile.

Charity was the only one who protested. "I don't think that's being fair to Todd," she said. My heart beat faster. "After all, he was winning before he abandoned the race to save his friend."

"Uh, thanks, Charity," I stammered. "That's nice of you to say, only . . ." Only I didn't want to be on the swim team anymore. Madame Dauphinee was taking just one boy, and I wasn't about to challenge Max—he already had enough reasons to want to kill the Toddlians. But I didn't seem to have a choice.

"Yes, Charity. That's a good point," Madame Dauphinee said, looking thoughtful. "We must remember that the WAVES is about sportsmanship first and winning second. This is a difficult decision, but decide I must. So the replacements for *les criminels* will be: for their exceptional athleticism, Max Loving and Charity Driscoll . . ."

Charity's face fell, and I felt a little disappointed,

despite myself. Still, I'd made my choice, and I'd rather keep Duddy alive than skip out on gym class any day.

Madame Dauphinee tapped her clipboard. "And in honor of the heroism and sacrifice shown here today, we'll mix things up a little and add a second boy rather than another girl! Todd Butroche—what a lovely French surname! Because you have touched my heart today, you will be the third new member of the WAVES."

Max threw his fist into the air. "I'm in! YEAH! I'm in! Good thing, because I would have totally mopped the floor with these losers if Dudboy hadn't decided to drown himself." He sneered at Duddy, who was chattering to Ike and Wendell, happily oblivious.

But Madame Dauphinee had heard Max's boast, and the sweetness went right out of her. "That is the quickest way to find yourself off the team, Mr. Loving. I have zero tolerance for unsportsmanlike conduct."

Max rolled his eyes and planted himself on the other side of Wendell, who scooched closer to Ike, causing us all to squish like sardines.

"Welcome aboard the WAVES!" Madame Dauphinee said as she shook our hands. "How are you feeling, Duddy?" she asked, looking intently into his eyes.

"A little seasick, but otherwise A-OK. I don't suppose the WAVES needs a mascot? I could be the Wakefield Walrus or something . . ." He barked a couple of times and clapped his hands like they were flippers.

Madame Dauphinee smiled. "Well, I don't—"

"What if I promised to wear floaties?" Duddy gave her his biggest grin.

She patted him on the head like he was a puppy. "Sorry, Duddy. I'm afraid you're going to have to stay on dry land until you've signed up for swimming lessons. But come *parler français avec moi* next semester, and I'll make you my special chocolate crêpes. I like your attitude!"

"Sure!" Duddy said, like that's what he'd hoped for all along.

"*Tres bien*, it's time to change and go home, everyone!" Madame Dauphinee shouted, waving us away with her clipboard. "Tryouts are over. *Au revoir!*"

Charity gave a last smile to the girls who were congratulating her and ran over to me. "I'm so psyched, Todd!" she said, shaking my hand. "It'll be nice to have a *friend* on the team!" She didn't let go of my hand, and I didn't let go of hers. But before I could congratulate her in return, Max interrupted our moment. He stood right beside her, glaring at me and growling like a grizzly.

To spend more time with Charity, I was going to have to spend more time with Max.

I could only hope to keep the Toddlians far, far away from the pool.

CHAPTER 8

As soon as we'd dried off, Duddy and I got ourselves out of the locker room. Max had trailed us as we dressed, threatening the usual: over-the-head wedgies, limb-from-limb dismemberment, squashing our skulls, and, my personal favorite, roasting us like suckling pigs with his brand-new blowtorch.

He'd followed us outside, but his big brother was there in his orange Camaro, so I survived to swim another day. Ike and Wendell were waiting for us under the big red maple by the bike rack. They'd prepared a solemn ceremony in honor of the saving of Duddy.

"Hi, guys!" I said, returning their Saki Salute. Wendell did a deep bow, his black sumo ponytail flipping him in the face. "Brave warrior," he said, seriously. "We thank you."

Ike scratched his armpits, giving me a full-blown Mongee-Poo victory dance, complete with a triple karate chop. "HOO HOO HI—"

"Not now, Ike," Wendell whispered. "This is a serious occasion. Our fellow warrior, Grand Dragon Master Scanlon, was nearly lost beneath the briny depths of the Wakefield Waters of Woe. Had it not been for the valiant self-sacrifice and bravery of Master Butroche, this would be a sad day indeed."

Ike wiped the smile off his face and nodded. "Indeed. Now, Sensei Nagee?"

"Now, my little monkey friend," Wendell replied, holding out his hand. Ike pulled some black rolled-up material out of Wendell's backpack and handed it to him.

Wendell went down on one knee and extended the roll to me. "With my humble compliments."

I unrolled a black T-shirt. "Ohmygosh! You can't give me this, Wendell. I know how much it cost!"

He waved his hand like he was shooing a fly. "A mere trifle compared to the life of a friend. Wear it well."

"Thanks! I will!" Right there in the schoolyard I ripped off my gray hoodie and reverently pulled on the limited-edition, artist-signed, straight-from-Japan, Koi Boy gold embroidered T-shirt. I'd been drooling over it since the first time I met Wendell and he had it on. *Suuuweeet!*

"That shirt is so cool!" Duddy said as we left the schoolyard and started walking home together. I was trying to up our speed; I couldn't wait to get to Lucy's and check on the Toddlians.

"You can say that again."

Duddy being Duddy, he said it again. "Ike and Wendell are the best," he added.

"Yeah." It had taken me a while to come around to Duddy's new buds, but now they were my buds, too. I looked over my shoulder at the pair I used to call the Dork Duo. Instead of their usual karate slashing, they walked away from Wakefield solemnly, like they were going to a funeral. Or more accurately, like they'd been spared from going to one. Wendell gave me one last Saki Salute as they headed in the other direction, down the street toward his house.

For real, those guys were growing on me.

When we turned onto our street, Olympia Avenue, Duddy grabbed my shoulder and said seriously, "Listen, Todd, I should really thank you for saving my life."

"You already did," I reminded him. "About a million times. Said you owed me a nacho mountain at Dave and Buster's, remember?"

"Oh, yeah." Duddy nodded. "Man, I love nachos." Then he paused, looking at his shoes and taking a deep breath. When he looked back up at me, his expression was dead serious. "So, uh, almost dying was kind of weird. My life didn't flash before my eyes or anything. But I did think two things: One, what will happen to my ant farm? And two, at least Max won't be able to kill me in gym class, because I'll already be dead." He giggled at his own joke.

But I didn't laugh. "Actually, Max won't have to take gym anymore either, since he's on the team with me." I shuddered.

Duddy shot me a sympathetic look and cleared his throat. "Hey! Speaking of, well, exercise, have you heard about the big dance at the community center?"

"No. Who cares about that?"

Duddy gave me kind of a sheepish look and started talking überfast. "Well, Ike and Wendell are planning on going. They said it's open to any kids who live in Wakefield, and it's this Friday, so I thought maybe we should go, too."

"I dunno, Dudster. I've never been to a dance before. I don't even know how to dance." *Don't want to learn either.*

"You break-dance!" Duddy said excitedly. "You've got awesome moves, Todd."

This was getting weird. "I can do the Worm. Kind of." I swallowed hard. I'd promised to teach the young Toddlians how to break-dance and had completely forgotten.

"Earth-to-Todd," Duddy said in a robot voice. "Come-in-Todd. Do-you-read-me?" When I didn't respond, Duddy took a big breath and said quickly, "Remember when I said I thought about two things when I was drowning? Well, actually there were three. Can I ask you something real important?"

I blinked at him. What was he saying? I looked around and saw we'd walked past my house and were right in front of Lucy's place. "Oh, hey! Hold that thought. I have to run in there and pick up the Toddlians."

By this point I was halfway up the driveway, but Duddy was still on the sidewalk. I turned to see what was wrong with him. His face said it all.

"Look, Dud, if you have to go that bad I'm sure Mrs. P won't mind if you use their bathroom." He was hopping back and forth on one foot, and his face was screwed up like he was about to explode. Duddy'd drunk a lot of pool water. I didn't want to clean up that mess. "C'mon, I'll ask her for you. She's nice. Totally bizarre, but nice."

Duddy skittered up the drive, still contorting his face. "Everything's cool," he said with a little shake.

"Are you gonna hurl?" I asked. "You could use the bathroom for that, too."

"Naw," he said in a helium-high voice. "Everything's cool."

Wow, he was being weird. But it *was* Duddy. Maybe nearly dying had made him even stranger than normal.

I rang the doorbell, and Lucy let us in. "Hey, Todd!" she said about half an inch from my face. "I'm really glad to see you."

"Uh, I think Duddy here—"

"Oh, hi, Duddy!" Lucy said, pulling him inside. "Great to see you, too! It's a party!" She snort-giggled, and I glanced at Duddy, whose face had turned fuchsia. Fluffy, the Pedotos' hairless cat, came up to us and rubbed our legs with his weird naked body. Duddy bent over to pet him. The cat hissed and shot off into the living room.

"He's fickle," Lucy explained as she led us down the hall. "Fluffy wanted to mark you with his scent, but he didn't like being touched back. He feels patronized, I think."

"I didn't know cats could be patriotic," Duddy blurted, and then blushed like he wished he'd never said it.

I chuckled awkwardly, and so did Lucy. Duddy just walked into Lucy's room and sat on the edge of her bed, shaking his head.

"Um, how are the Toddlians?" I asked.

Lucy gave me a big grin. "Well, let me show you! Todd, welcome to Wee Peeps Wellness Center, or WPWC for short! Just look at this exercise equipment I made for the Toddlians today. A stationary bicycle made out of paper clips, some weights from a toothpick and pencil erasers, a treadmill . . . Now Toddlandia can have its very own gym!" Lucy laid the WPWC on her desk and handed me a set of micro-glasses.

I put them on and bent to eye level with the WP Whatever. Some of the Toddlians cheered when they saw me. Lewis was jogging on a rubber-band treadmill that was powered by Persephone turning a tiny toothpick handle.

"That way they both get the benefit of exercise." Lucy said. "Cardio for him, upper body for her. Cool, huh?"

I nodded. Creating the gym had probably taken Lucy all day. Meanwhile I hadn't even found time to teach the little guys the Worm. "Hi, Lewis! How's the workout?" I asked, hoping he was having fun, at least.

He hopped off the treadmill and bowed. "Hail . . . Great Todd . . . live forever," he panted. "Lewis is . . . so glad to . . . see you are well. I've been . . . lifting weights!" He grunted and struck a muscleman pose. Persephone whistled, and I cracked up.

"Howdy, Persephone!" I said. "Didja miss me?" But she didn't answer, just stomped to the edge of the gym and scowled at me like she'd been guzzling sugarless lemonade.

Now what have I done? I just got here, for crying out loud. Girls made no sense whatsoever.

Lucy proved it by pulling me to her window and whispering, "Todd, I'm worried about the Toddlians . . . and *you.*" She leaned in so close our foreheads nearly touched. "Are you certain you wouldn't like me to take the Toddlians for a while? Or we could set up the camera on your laptop so you could check on them remotely. I could, too, for that matter. Then, if they were in distress I could run over and assist them."

I stepped back. "You mean *spying*? No! That's . . . that's insane. This isn't 1984! There are laws against that kind of thing, Lucy!"

Lucy arched her black eyebrows and said excitedly, "You're an Orwell fan too? Wasn't *1984* amazing? He was such a visionary!"

"Wait, *1984* is a book?" I asked. "I just thought there was a lot of spying and stuff in the year 1984. You know, because people always say that . . ." I shut up before I sounded any stupider. "Anyway," I said, picking up the shoebox, "I'll just take them home now. Thanks for babysitting." I fit the gym inside the box and grabbed the slipper off her bed.

Lucy grabbed my arm and leaned in close, like she was telling me a secret. Duddy made a weird noise, causing us both to look up.

He looked all pink and uncomfortable. "Uh, excuse me. I . . . sneezed."

I'd never heard Duddy sneeze like that, but whatever. Lucy turned back to me. "Yanno, Todd, I can't help thinking that the Toddlians need to further their educations—be exposed to learned people. Herman, for example—"

"And by 'learned' you mean yourself?" I stepped back.

"Mm-hmm. Well, no, not merely myself. I didn't mean that the way it sounded, like you weren't capable . . . I just think they need their horizons broadened. They need to meet philosophers and scientists—"

"No!" I yelled, causing her to flinch. "Are you crazy? That's the last thing the Toddlians need. The only way to keep them safe is to keep them hidden. You, Duddy, me, Max, and those stupid eighth graders Spud and Dick, who've hopefully forgotten about them by now—those are the only people who can know that they exist, and that's already way too many people! Nobody else can find out. Got it?"

"Okay, I got it, I got it." Lucy sighed.

Duddy glanced up at me, then studied his shoes and turned pink again. *Gee, thanks, Dud.* What was *up* with him? I set the Toddlians gently on Lucy's desk and plopped down next to him on the bed.

Lucy still looked confused, but I wasn't about to budge. "The Toddlians are my responsibility," I said, "and I have to protect them from outsiders." I'd learned that much, at least.

Nobody said anything for a minute. I had to break the awkward silence. Then I remembered . . . "So, Duddy," I said, turning to him, "what was that big, important question you wanted to ask me outside?"

He stared at me in horror, his face so red it was almost purple. "I . . . have no idea what you're talking about, Todd."

"Sure, you remember," I helped. "You said there was a third thing you thought of in the pool, but you didn't tell it to me at first and—"

"No I didn't!" he squeaked. "You must have been hearing things." He looked desperately at Lucy. "Todd must have water in his ears, because I have no idea what he's talking about."

"Duddy," Lucy said gently, "are you feeling okay?"

"I feel fine!" he squealed as he jumped up. "But I have to go now . . . and, erm . . . feed my ants! Yeah. Poor little guys are probably starving. Bye!"

Duddy was down the hall and had slammed the front door before either Lucy or I could say anything. I shrugged and looked at her. "Well, that was weird."

"Yeah," she said. "It's also potentially dangerous. I'm afraid he's overfeeding those ants." Lucy put her face right next to my ear. "Did Duddy say you are suffering from a little *Otitis externa*? Because a mixture of fifty percent alcohol and fifty vinegar would probably dry that right up. I can mix it up and drop it in for you. Of course, suction helps as well. Hmmm. Why don't you lie down on your side—"

"NO!" I shouted, jumping up. "Thanks and everything, but I need to grab the Toddlians and get home. I brought some sweaty socks from gym class today that

I'm sure they'd love to gorge themselves on." I carefully placed the Toddlians back in the shoebox and shut the lid, hoisting it under my arm. "Anyway, thanks for watching them while I figured out what to do about Max. Gottagonow. Bye."

I got out of there and across the street to my house before any other weird stuff could happen.

Not that having an entire civilization of tiny people who lived off your dirt was weird or anything.

CHAPTER 9

LEWIS

Once we were safely back in Toddlandia, Herman clicked on Todd's flashlight, which illuminated the dark and dusty expanse beneath Todd's bed. He had called all Toddlians for a special meeting to be held in the very place where our race began: upon the hallowed sock. The flashlight focused on an enormous object that was mysteriously draped with a pair of Todd's unsoiled undergarments.

Herman positioned himself in the center of the light, held up his arms, and spoke. "My fellow Toddlians, you know that I have been working on a Big Plan. We have reached a point in our history that will decide the fate of future generations. You must all admit that the recent negligence of our god has left us no choice."

No choice? I didn't like the tone of Herman's address. What action was he about to propose without so much as a vote?

Herman continued. "Recently, Todd's paternal person was laboring underneath his automobile, and I happened to be doing a little research in the garage room. A song was playing on the wireless transmission device, and I felt the words to be quite apropos to our current crisis." Herman cleared his throat and sang in a low voice, "You've gotta know when to hold 'em . . . Know when to fold 'em . . ."

"Ooooo," chorused the other Toddlians, applauding.

Persephone tossed her hat into the air and whooped, "Now that's tellin' 'em, Hermie!"

Herman continued, his pale face full of resolve. "It is my humble opinion that it is time to do as the omens say, and *run*. We must gather up our courage, along with representatives of the other species we wish to preserve, and embark on a new era of Toddlian exploration." At this he signaled to the Toddlians holding the edges of the underpants. They pulled the covering off and revealed an immense and beautiful . . . boat?!?

A cheer rose from the awestruck crowd, and I forgot my frustration and joined in the admiration. I'd known since the Fly Attack that occurred just before Todd brought us to Lucy's that Herman was working on a new sailing vessel, but I was unprepared for the magnificence of this one. The boat was as high as the Meeting Hut (the tallest building in Toddlandia), and about half as long as Todd's laptop computer.

"Welcome aboard *The Exodus*, our very own ark of exploration and preservation!" Herman led us on a tour of the vessel, and I was momentarily dazed by its grandeur. "You will note that the peaked roof is made of beautiful baseball cards. Never fear—the waxy coating has been thoroughly tested for water resistance. These sides and this door are constructed of wooden matches and toothpicks, respectively. They are securely pitched with bubble gum mined from Todd's sneakers."

"Oooooo!"

Herman gave a slight bow and then led us below deck into the hold of the ark, which was lined with rows of large compartments divided by matchstick walls. "Here are enough stalls and enclosures to hold a male and female of each of the 'critters' Persephone and her helpers have been collecting. There is also room to store the foodstuffs each species (including ours) needs to survive a journey over water."

That snapped me back to reason. "A journey over water?" I repeated, dumbstruck. "Just where are we going?"

Herman stopped gesturing and looked at me

curiously. "Why, wherever the current takes us, in hopes of finding another god!"

"NO!" I shouted, mortified. "That is NOT how the story Lucy told us ended. Don't you remember how the *same* previously offended god welcomed the faithful humans out of the boat, received their offerings, and accepted them back into his care?"

Herman was in a rare state of speechlessness.

I continued with my case. "Don't you recall how he set a prismatic bow in the clouds to reassure the human race that there would never, ever be another such flood?"

Some of my people murmured in agreement. But Herman did not look convinced. He weaved through the crowded deck to where I stood, and placed his hand on my shoulder. "Lewis, my friend, I know that is the conclusion of the biblical account. But we . . . we . . ." His gaze fell, and he bit his lower lip.

"You were saying?"

Herman's eyes met mine, and they were full of sadness. "Given his recent neglect, do you think Todd will even pursue us if we flee?"

My heart burned within me. How had Herman so entirely lost faith in the Great One? "Of course he will!" I insisted. "Do you doubt his love?"

I felt a gentle squeeze on my shoulder. "Lew," Persephone pleaded, "take off yer blinders. Cain't you see how Todd's been treatin' us lately? You ain't had a civil word from him in weeks. Somethin' or *somebody* else has hogtied his heart, and there jest ain't room in it for us anymore."

I couldn't speak. I knew there was truth to her words, but oh, the ache they left in my soul!

A fire deep within me was flickering and about to die, and I was losing the strength to fan its feeble flame. I trudged to the exit ramp, turning to take one more look at the ark that would sail us away from the only home we had ever known . . . away from *Todd.*

Persephone, ever one for action, was shimmying up to one of the rafters. She waved her hat. "Captain Herman," she called. "Whaddaya say we see if this ol' gal is seaworthy?"

Herman saluted solemnly. "Aye, aye. But for this aquatic trial we shall need to procure an able assistant. Now where is Lewis?"

Ironically, I was the one appointed to be the Toddlians' ambassador to The Adorable One They Call Daisy. She was, it seemed, our only possible ally. Herman and Persephone were not convinced she was completely unsympathetic to her elder brother, but *I* was. Still, I was not to tell her the real purpose of the *Exodus* experiment.

My conscience smote me with every step I took to the nursery. *Trai-tor. Trai-tor. Trai-tor.*

Finally I slipped under the closed door.

I knew this to be "Daisy's nap time," per her unsupportive mother. I also knew that Daisy created her most exquisite art during these hours of unobserved freedom.

When I approached, The Adorable One was putting the final touches on an expressionist painting. She was coloring an undulating sunset on her wall, using Todd's orange permanent marker. Under the blazing sky was a waving image with hands on either side of its face. The frantic face had wide eyes and an O-shaped mouth.

The picture perfectly captured my present pent-up frustration. I was too moved to express my admiration.

Daisy spat out her Binky and spoke in my native language. "Do you remember this one, Lewis?" What sounded like burbling nonsense to her human family was actually fluent Toddlian.

"Edvard Munch's *The Scream of Nature*?" I volunteered. I remembered it from her Famous Paintings for Preschoolers flash card set.

She nodded and tilted her head, turning a critical eye on her endeavor. "It would have looked better in pastels, but that's the price you pay for eating your sidewalk chalk."

I cleared my throat and climbed atop her musical table in order to better communicate. "Adorable One, I have come to ask a favor."

She picked up a yellow marker and scowled. "Succotash! I've bitten the end off this one, too! I must remember to stop doing that." Daisy rummaged around in the cup that held Todd's markers, choosing a red one. "What was your favor, little Lewis? Does the Toddlian library need another etching? I'd love to try a tiny Rembrandt. Perhaps *The Rat Catcher*?"

"That would be lovely, but I come on a more urgent errand. My friend Herman has built a remarkable boat for us to . . . take on an extended voyage. But we need to make certain it is seaworthy. Could you help us?"

Daisy's face broke into a grin that looked a bit devious. She rubbed her pudgy hands together and said, "Hee hee hee. *Excellent*. Meet me in the bathroom in fifteen minutes."

It took every last Toddlian to haul *The Exodus* into the bathroom by cotton threads from Todd's frayed old Y-fronts. When we finally reached our destination, Daisy was waiting. Upon seeing the ark, she cooed and cackled and did her happy spinning stomp dance.

The Adorable One picked up the ark and studied it. "What unusual lines, Herman. What craftsmanship!" Then she gave it a sniff and said, "Is that Dubble Bubble between the planks? Your ingenuity knows no bounds!"

Daisy carefully set *The Exodus* on the fluffy pink toilet seat cover, then picked up a red toy boat from the floor. "Note the differences of the two crafts." She held both boats aloft. "My red plastic tugboat tubby toy is a mere sham of a ship compared to the detail and character of your fine watercraft. It simply delights the senses! But we must set aside its aesthetic qualities; the real test will be how she sails!"

Her Adorableness set the boats on the bathtub edge and flipped up the drain lever. She turned the cold handle. Water shot out of the faucet, and she broke into a ritual chant about an itsy-bitsy spider, which gave the enterprise a chilling and mysterious accompaniment. Persephone readied her lasso, in case we encountered the beast.

Herman had filled stretchy tan bags (made from nylon stockings he had discovered one night as they soaked in the bathroom sink) with grains of sand from Daisy's sandbox to represent the different weights of the creatures that would be joining us on our trip. Daisy placed the sandbags in the hold and then allowed us to climb onto her hand and ascend the gangplank of *The Exodus*.

We filed onto the deck. I was careful to find a place near the side where I could grip the floss handles that lined the rails. Once we were all safely on board, Herman waved to Daisy. The Adorable One shrieked with unrestrained glee as she dropped us in the rapidly rising water.

My stomach flipped as the boat fell into the bathtub.

We hit the water with a mighty *SPLASH!* that sent us all rolling across the deck. I crawled to the nearest floss handles and pulled myself to my knees as the boat plummeted up, then dove down through the choppy waves. As soon as I was able to stand, my neighbor slammed into me, knocking me off my feet again. Cold water sloshed over the side, dousing me and everyone else on board. We were all screaming for mercy, and I, for one, was ready to get back on dry linoleum and scrap the entire operation.

The boat careened crazily in circles, whirling dangerously close to the violent waterfall gushing out of the faucet. The contents of my stomach lurched into my mouth with the mad spinning. The retchfest that followed was most unpleasant. Apparently I was not the only Toddlian experiencing seasickness!

We cried for Daisy to turn off the water, but she was singing "Row, Row, Row Your Boat" at such an ear-splitting volume that there was just no chance she could hear us. Soon the inevitable happened: the boat spun under the cascade of the faucet and began taking on water. The thundering gush pummeled our craft, tilting the deck wildly downward and hurling several of us overboard. I screamed, clinging to the floss handle and yelling for my fellow unfortunates to hang on to me. We made a Toddlian chain, and the last of us grabbed hold of the ship's helm, which was spinning uncontrollably.

"Throw the sandbags overboard!" Herman cried as the ark spun away from the faucet. That was easier said than done, since the boat was listing heavily on the port side. We frantically tossed what bags we could over the sides of the boat, heaving with nausea all the while.

Daisy, meanwhile, did not notice our plight. "MERRILY, MERRILY, MERRILY," she crooned, turning in mad circles like a dervish. "LIFE IS BUT A DREAM!"

By this time the water was even with the top of the tub. We were rushing at a horrifying speed to the edge. Our doom seemed imminent!

"I don't want to die!" little Milly cried. We clung to each other, tumbling down the deck toward the churning water . . .

"GENTLY DOWN THE STREAM!" our oblivious helper caterwauled.

Even if we managed to stay aboard the ark, the water was now up to our necks, and the boat was careening toward the edge of the bathtub—and with it, our certain doom.

"GREAT TODD, HAVE MERCY ON US!" I screamed into the growing mist.

But it was not Great Todd who saved us.

It was a rubber ducky. Or more precisely, The Adorable One *via* a rubber ducky. With her song over, she finally heard our cries. She set the yellow duck toy in the water and then held it steady while we clambered onto its flat back. When my turn came to climb aboard, the back and wings were full, so I wrapped my arms around a plastic tail feather and held on for dear life, my legs dangling in the frigid water. Persephone helped the weaker Toddlians out of the sinking ark and onto the duck's head. She was the last to board the life craft and took her perch upon the bill.

Daisy, humming happily, lifted the duck out of the water and set it gently on the toilet lid. We jumped off and began to dry our shivering selves on the fluffy fibers of the toilet seat cover.

But no sooner were we rescued than the still-running water splashed over the edges of the bathtub, creating another massive, rushing waterfall. We were safe on the toilet seat, but the sound was overpowering! In a few moments we gasped as the sodden *Exodus* plunged over the edge and floated toward the toilet, coming to rest behind it. Daisy danced and splashed with wild abandon in the water that now covered the bathroom floor. But her rejoicing was short-lived.

Within seconds, The Adorable One's mother threw open the door and stood frozen with a laundry basket balanced on her hip. Water gushed over her feet as she surveyed the flooded bathroom. Her normally lovely face contorted into something inhuman and evil. We had been shivering with cold, but now, we quaked from fear.

"DAISY LORRAINE BUTROCHE!" the mother bellowed. "*What. Are. You. Doing?*" She waded through the water to turn the faucet off and open the drain and then attempted to pick up the now howling toddler with her free arm.

Daisy transformed herself into a wet noodle and slid out of her mother's grasp to the floor, where she suddenly regained use of her limbs, kicking and pounding the wet linoleum.

The mother slapped herself in the forehead. "Do you know there's water pouring from the basement ceiling? DO YOU?"

Daisy's response was to crawl to the wall and grab the towel from the rack. She then gave a terrifying shriek and threw it into the bathtub.

The mother's eyes widened, and her nostrils flared. "You stop that right now, young lady, or no *Yo Gabba Gabba!* for a . . . a week!"

Daisy flung herself backward, thrashing about like the proverbial fish out of water. Which was ironic, since she was in quite a lot of water.

"*Okay then, let's try a month!*" the mother screeched. We couldn't hear the rest of what she said because by this point we were covering our ears to keep them from bleeding. The mother mopped up the floor, despite the flailing baby, then somehow managed to haul her to the nursery—to change her sopping clothes, I presumed.

We began our trembling descent from the toilet, sliding down Persephone's floss lasso one at a time.

"AAAUUURRRGGGHHH!" the mother screeched from the nursery. Had she seen Daisy's latest masterpiece, *The Scream of Nature*? I paused in my descent to catch my breath and consider the irony of the situation. Poor, unappreciated Adorable One. If only she did not possess such a fiery artistic temperament . . .

The commotion from the nursery sped our departure. We doggedly made our escape from the madness down the hallway. Todd's room seemed like a million miles away, and we were extremely weak from our recent ordeal.

Herman was first to speak. "I think we will all agree that Daisy is too unstable in nature to be a reliable god, just in case anyone had been considering appealing to Her Adorableness."

We were all in agreement on that point, at least. He continued, "While this was an uncomfortable experience—"

"Uncomfortable?" Persephone interrupted. "Lemme see: we chucked our grub all over each other, swallowed enough water to choke a steer, and durn nearly drowned at the hands of a harebrained baby. Yep, that's mighty *uncomfortable*, Herman!"

Herman acknowledged Persephone's complaint with a solemn nod, then said, "The good news is, the experiment was not in vain. I have learned valuable lessons about the construction flaws of *The Exodus* and feel confident that once I make repairs, she will sail beautifully. We will recover the vessel once Todd's maternal person is asleep. Luckily, it landed behind the toilet, and we must hope it will remain there undiscovered."

I summoned my courage while the recent terror was a fresh memory. "I do not mean to subvert Herman's leadership," I said to my fellow travelers, "but surely the most valuable lesson we've learned this afternoon is how dangerous it is to act hastily."

There were murmurs of agreement, and I glanced at the weary Herman. His jaw clenched, but he did not reply.

I pressed my point. "Herman, did you yourself not once say, 'Quick decisions are unsafe decisions'?"

He sighed and nodded. "Though I owe the sentiment to Sophocles."

I walked backward through the hallway fibers, addressing my friends. "All I'm asking for is another opportunity to reason with Todd. I feel sure he will see our distress and act accordingly. Please? Just give Todd one more chance."

CHAPTER 10

The next afternoon, I stepped out of the locker room, took a deep breath of the chlorine-soaked air, and looked around for Charity. She waved me over from the bleachers. I waved back and started toward her.

But Max beat me to Charity's side. He swaggered up to her in his Speedo and . . . *sparkly feelers?* . . . and started chatting her up.

Charity rolled her eyes at him. She looked like she needed rescuing. I shuffled her way a few steps, until I was close enough to hear what Max was spewing.

And he was *literally* spewing. "The best thing about Venessa is that she's a bee, so she can sting her enemies but she never dies. Did you know that when bees sting, all their little guts get stuck . . . no, *sucked* out with their stingers? But Valerie's not like that, she's got a super-natural stinker . . . *stinger*." He stopped to swallow his spit and wipe his mouth with the back of his hand.

I think Charity would have laughed if it weren't for the spit that had landed on her arm. She dried it with her towel and opened her mouth to say something, but Max cut her off. "Sorry about that, it's just that I get sooo excited when I'm talking about *Dragon Sensor*, I kind of lose it a little!"

"*Dragon* Sensei," Charity corrected.

"Right," Max said, nodding so hard the headband slid off. He put it back on and said, "Maybe you could help me spruce up my Veronica costume. So far all I've got are these antennae and a pair of my mom's pantyhose. I thought I could maybe stretch those over some tennis rackets or something for the wings."

Veronica? What was he talking about? Then it hit me: Max Loving was trying to play . . . *Vespa?!*

Charity shot me a *Can you believe this guy?* glance. Her blue eyes were shining, and I could tell she was laughing inside as hard as I was.

"That's all great, Max," she said over her shoulder as she bounded down the bleachers. "But I really want to talk to Todd now." Charity grabbed my hand and led me toward the cluster of kids who were warming up. I saw Max look my way and punch his fist into his palm. His raging bull face looked pretty silly under his pom-pom antennae, but I didn't smile; I'd felt that fist around my neck.

Charity leaned over, causing her hair to tumble across my shoulder. I closed my eyes and breathed in the tropical smell of her shampoo.

"So," she said, twisting her hair into a shiny rope, "I thought Max seemed a little confused about a few things, didn't you?" She straightened up and winked at me. I just grinned like a goober and watched her pink-tipped fingers hide all that hair under her silver swim cap. "And those antennae!" she whispered with dancing eyes. "I could hardly keep a straight face!"

Her nose wrinkled up so cute when she giggled. I wanted to stand there with her forever, just the two of us making fun of Max. But then Madame Dauphinee pierced through my personal paradise with a blast from her whistle. "Boys in first, *s'il vous plaît!*"

I must've looked confused because Charity whispered in my ear, "If you please." Her breath tickled me all the way down to my toes. I felt like I was floating on a fluffy cloud as I snapped on my goggles and hopped into the water.

As soon as I got lined up in my lane, Max reached over and shoved his hands into my back, pushing me into the pool. Water shot into my sinuses, chlorine burning all the way. I came up gasping and sputtering.

Max leaned across the rope separating our lanes and said with mock sincerity, "Oh, that was an accident. I'm sooo sorry, Buttrock."

I pretended I was Mongee-Poo and shot radiated "sludge" water out my nostrils and into Max's face. "And I'm sorry too, Max. It's so sad Charity didn't buy your whole 'I'm really into *Dragon Sensei*' act."

Max flinched like he was going to lunge at me, but then he seemed to realize that wasn't going to work and gave a nonchalant shrug. "Doesn't matter." He slid his goggles from his cap to his eyes and gave me an evil grin. "I've got a little surprise planned that even Charity won't be able to resist."

With a curl of the lip, he splashed me in the face and then started swimming laps. I studied the waving blue *W* on the pool bottom. What could Max mean by *a little surprise*?

Practice went surprisingly well (except for Max trying to mess with me every thirty seconds) and was nearly done when suddenly I heard Max call out, "Madame D? I need to go do something."

"Can this wait, Monsieur Loving?" Madame Dauphinee glanced at the clock on the wall. "Practice is almost over."

He shrugged. "Oh, sure. People pee in the water all the time, right?"

A bunch of girls screamed. Madame Dauphinee

scowled at Max and pointed in the direction of the boys'
locker room. Max took his time hefting himself out of
the pool, and from the way he casually strolled into the
locker room, it was obvious he didn't have to go *that* bad.

For a few minutes I forgot about Max and focused on
the freestyle drill Madame Dauphinee had me working on.

"You are made like a chocolate éclair, Monsieur
Butroche—slim in the middle." Madame Dauphinee
flicked the water and made a swooshing rocket sound.
"A tiny torpedo, that's what you are, my friend. Now,
swim! With more rotation!"

Though I was a total klutz on land, I was surprisingly
pretty graceful in the water. It had to be natural talent,
because I'd only made it through the Bitty Beta level in
swim lessons at the Y.

Madame Dauphinee told me to keep practicing and
asked Maya to watch over us while she went into her
office to fix somebody's busted goggles. I'd just done my
flip turn and was starting into another lap when someone poked me in the side. I popped up to see Charity
next to me, her mouth wide open. I whirled around in
the water to see what she was pointing at. My mouth
dropped open, too.

All the girls were screeching and scrambling to get
out of the pool. A shimmery, oily film danced over the
surface of the water, trailing away from Max, who stood
at the edge of the pool, draped in a grungy green hooded

bath towel. Raising the sides like bat wings, Max threw back his head, cackling crazily. "I TOLD YOU I WOULD BE BACK, OORA! NOW I WILL VANQUISH MY ENEMIES WITH WAVES OF FLAAAAME!"

"'SharkTruese's Showdown,'" I whispered. Those lines were straight out of my favorite *Dragon Sensei* episode! Max had got it right for once.

Charity gulped. "Which means he's about to . . . AAAUUUGGGHHH!" she shrieked as Max bent over the water's edge, slowly lowering a lit match to the oil.

WHOOMF! The water beneath Max exploded into little tongues of orange flame that started licking up the trail of shiny stuff. The fire wasn't very big . . . yet. The people who were near the flames screamed and jumped out of the pool like it was full of piranhas. Kids came running out of the weight room to see what the excitement was all about. It was total chaos.

Charity scrambled up the ladder with me right behind her. She tore up the cement to the other end of the pool, ripped the robe-towel off Max, and dunked it in the water, smothering the flames.

"What kind of nutcase *are* you?" Charity yelled, shoving Max's chest. He wobbled a bit and then regained his balance. "Are you trying to kill us all?" She leaned over the pool's edge and beat the small fire into oblivion.

Madame Dauphinee barreled out of her office, and the whole team rushed her and started shouting.

"Loving tried to set us on fire!" a skinny kid accused, pointing at Max, who swiveled his head around and sneered like a trapped tiger.

"The fire was at least six feet high," somebody lied.

"Was not, it never even actually ignited!" somebody else insisted. That comment about started World War III, with most kids agreeing that however small, there *had* been flames.

Madame Dauphinee quivered all over, and her face turned bright red. She took a deep breath and blew her whistle, which was as good as a mute button on a remote. Everyone took a big step back. Even Max looked nervous.

I wasn't sure what Coach Dauphinee was saying, but it sounded like she was swearing in French. When she calmed down enough to speak English, she pointed up into Max's face and backed him onto a bleacher, talking the whole time. "I'm not sure what just happened, young man, but since you're the only one holding matches, I assume you tried to set my swimmers on fire. I have ZERO TOLERANCE for such behavior, and I'll have you know that if you don't want a police escort out of here, you will never darken these waters with your presence again. You are no longer one of the WAVES. Place your cap and goggles in your locker, then leave the building."

She stood on her tiptoes, and he bent away from her, plopping onto the bleacher. "And if this behavior keeps up, don't think I won't have you expelled just like I did your trouble-making big brother."

Max's eyes were huge, and he seemed truly terrified. Madame Dauphinee whirled around and faced the rest of her shocked swimmers. With a shaking hand she smoothed her black bun, then waved us away. "*Allez vous-en!* Go home! Practice is postponed until further notice." She pulled the whistle off and wound its white cord around her hands distractedly, muttering, "I need a Xanax . . ." Then more loudly she added, "I mean, I need some towels and a bucket. I should start skimming the lighter fluid out of the pool."

The kids scattered in all directions. I offered to help clean up, but Madame Dauphinee shooed me off, her eyes glazed over like she wasn't really seeing me. "*Merci*, Todd. But this mess is beyond both of us. We aren't exactly equipped to handle pyromaniacs around here." She let out a weird, loud laugh, and I slowly backed away.

I hoped Max hadn't broken Madame Dauphinee already.

I mean, I hadn't even gotten to taste her crêpes.

Thankfully, Max had left by the time I got to the locker room.

"Good thinking in there," I said to Charity when I

caught up to her in front of the school. She was sitting on a stone bench with her head leaned against the trunk of a tree.

"Oh, yeah. Thanks." She looked pretty shook up too.

"Are you okay?" I asked. "Sorry about all of that. Max is totally—"

"A moron?" she said, jumping up. "Max Loving. What kind of name is that, even?"

"I know, right? It's like he got named on Opposite Day."

At that moment I was treated to something amazing: Charity's laugh. The sound was heavenly; it sounded just like the tokens falling when you won on the Coin Pusher at Dave and Buster's.

Charity thinks I'm funny!

And then something even more amazing happened. "Hey," she said, "let's hang out and play some *Dragon Sensei*! I need to release some energy."

Was I dreaming this? Did the prettiest girl in school, maybe in the entire city, just ask *me* if I wanted to have a *Dragon Sensei* battle jam? I nodded, and we started walking toward my street. But then I remembered the Toddlians and how I'd just insisted to Lucy that no one else could find out about them. *That means even girls with tinkly laughs and hair like golden waterfalls . . .*

"Oh," I said, trying to sound casual, "but could we go to my friend Duddy's house? He's like the absolute grand master of all things *Dragon Sensei*. Plus our weapons and costumes are stored in his basement."

Charity smiled and agreed, so we strolled slowly down Olympia Avenue, talking about our favorite episodes and characters. I knew I was only twelve, but still, I was pretty sure this was one of those memories I'd look back on and smile about when I was eighty. The October sky was as blue as Charity's eyes, the air was crisp and clear, and the trees were . . . well, Boston is famous for its beautiful fall leaves. Funny, I'd never really noticed them before, even though Mom loaded us into the van every October to go "leaf-peeping."

It got quiet for a minute, so I pointed at my house. "That's where I live."

She stopped and studied it. "Nice place. Maybe next time we can go to *your* house."

I felt my face warming up as I tried to imagine her inside my house, in my room even. Would it be enough to hide the Toddlians? It just made me nervous . . . "That'd be cool. I should warn you, though. My baby sister Daisy is a living nightmare."

"You have a baby sister?" she squealed. "I loooove babies! Is she cute?"

"Well . . ." I didn't usually think of the Toddling Terror in those terms.

"Of course she's cute," Charity answered for me. "All babies are cute. Besides," she said, glancing sideways at me, "she has *you* for a brother."

Wait, was Charity calling me cute? My face burned, and I couldn't speak.

Luckily, by that time we'd reached Duddy's house.

"He's out," Duddy's sister Erin said as soon as she answered the bell.

"Can you tell us where he went?" Charity asked as I tried to peer into the hallway.

"Lucy Pedoto's house," she replied, shrugging her bony shoulders. Duddy's sister looked just like Duddy, but stretched out and with long hair. She must have noticed my bewildered expression because she quickly added, "Yeah, I don't know why he's there either." Then she slammed the door.

That made zero sense. Duddy never visited Lucy without me.

Charity turned to me. "Maybe we should just go to your house."

"*No!* Um, I mean, Duddy is *really* good at role-playing," I said. "Maybe we can just go to Lucy's and see what's up?"

Charity looked skeptical. "Who's Lucy, anyway?"

"Just my neighbor," I said, turning around and heading toward Lucy's. After a second, Charity followed.

"All right."

When we got to the Pedotos', I knocked on the front door. Mrs. Pedoto opened it, giving us one of her warm welcomes. "Well, hellooo, Todd! And who's this you've brought with you?"

Charity extended her hand and smiled. "I'm Charity Driscoll. Nice to meet you."

Mrs. Pedoto was clearly impressed with Charity's manners. "I'm sure Lucy will be delighted to see you, Charity." She patted a couple of bar stools. "Why don't you two have a seat while I find you a little snack."

Mrs. Pedoto dug around in the fridge, and Charity looked at me with raised eyebrows. "Gosh, we're not really . . ." I began, but Mrs. Pedoto had already gathered a tray of her "famous" gluten-free molasses ginger snaps, which were as hard as hockey pucks.

We gnawed politely on the cookies while Mrs. Pedoto asked Charity a list of questions: "You don't sound like you're from Boston; are you new in town? How do you feel about going to public school? In Florida, did you ever encounter an alligator in your plumbing, or is that just an urban legend?"

Finally Mrs. Pedoto released us from interrogation, and we walked down the hall to find Lucy's bedroom door open. When Charity and I entered, Lucy and Duddy were bent over her lab table, wearing goggles and adjusting some kind of laser beam.

"Uh, hi, guys," I stammered when they didn't notice us.

A red-faced Duddy raised his goggles and took in Charity and me. "Er, hey, Todd! Charity. I'm just helping Lucy build her, uh . . . caesarean clock."

"*Cesium* clock," Lucy corrected gently. She glanced at me, then shot a dubious look at Charity, who'd walked over to investigate. "It's an atomic clock."

Charity pointed to the digital clock on Lucy's night-stand. "Why do you need an atomic clock? What's wrong with that one?"

Lucy gave Charity the once-over, clearly unimpressed. "I'm sorry, you are . . . ?"

Charity looked her right in the eye. "Charity Driscoll. My family just moved into town, and I'm on the swim team with Todd. Pleased to meet you." She held out her hand, and Lucy reluctantly grabbed the tips of her fingers for a limp shake.

"Ahem. Sorry. There's nothing *wrong* with this clock, per se, but for the most precise time you need an atomic clock. Cesium clocks keep time better than the earth's rotation—"

"Better than the stars!" Duddy chimed in.

Lucy smiled at her pupil. "Let me break it down for you guys." She rolled her whiteboard over and went into full geek mode, filling it up with scientific lingo and numbers. I couldn't follow her at all, and Charity looked totally lost, but Dudster grinned and nodded like "genius" was his middle name.

Seriously, what is he doing here?

"I'd hoped to build a rubidium atomic clock," Lucy said. "But that would have been a complete waste of time since cesium clocks are more accurate."

Duddy nodded excitedly. "Tell them how accurate."

Lucy pointed to a ginormous number. "Cesium atoms emit microwaves that oscillate, or 'tick,' nine billion, one hundred ninety-two million, six hundred thirty-one thousand, seven hundred seventy times a second; they're only off once every three million years."

Charity whistled. "Wow, that's pretty accurate. Are you a member of Mensa or something?"

Lucy raised an eyebrow like Mensa was for losers. I knew for a fact she had aced the entrance test when she was nine and a half. "I just value accuracy, Charlotte," she huffed.

"Charity," Duddy, Charity, and I all said at once.

"Charity means 'love,'" Charity added, sending me a dimpled smile.

"Oh, really?" Lucy replied, fiddling with one of her lasers. "I think, more accurately, it means helping those who can't take care of themselves."

Charity's eyes flashed, and her full lips shrunk into a straight line.

Duddy blundered on, oblivious as ever. "Well, if there's one thing Charity doesn't need help in, it's swimming. She's absolutely *amazing* in the water! Isn't she, Todd?"

"She's from Florida," I said again stupidly, like that explained everything. "We were wondering if you wanted to play *Dragon Sensei*, Duddy. But I guess you're busy."

"OH!" Duddy shouted, jumping up and pointing to the closet. "Charity, you *have* to see Lucy's Vespa costume! It is THE COOLEST THING EVER! Isn't it, Todd?"

I couldn't argue with that. "It has hologram wings and a light-up stinger."

Charity's eyebrows went up. "I've heard about this costume. May I see it?"

Lucy jerked her head at the closet. "It's hanging in there." She turned her back on us and scribbled more scientific gibberish on her whiteboard. Charity looked confused.

"So what do you think?" I said to Duddy. "Wanna have a little battle jam?"

"Well . . ." Duddy walked over to the closet, found the costume, and laid it out on Lucy's bed.

Charity whistled again. "That is amazing! Lucy, would you model it?"

Lucy shrugged. "I mean . . . I'm kind of . . ."

"Come on, put it on, Lucy," I coaxed. "We can all go over to Duddy's and role-play." I turned to Charity. "You can borrow Duddy's Saki costume. It's sweet."

Lucy cleared her throat. "I don't think so. I should really get back to work." She looked from me to Charity, her gaze cooling. "I'm really invested in this clock right now. But you guys feel free to go play games."

"Um, ooookay . . . Since you're not going, could Charity wear your Vespa suit?" I turned to Charity, who was sitting next to me. I didn't know why Lucy was being so weird, but at least the three of us could still play. "I know Vespa's not your favorite character, but you'd look really good in it."

I looked at Charity eagerly, but the room had gone weirdly silent.

What did I say?

Suddenly Lucy swooped down and snatched the costume out of Charity's hands. "It needs some repair work before it's ready to be worn," she snapped. "Besides, I don't think it would be big enough to fit Charlene."

"Charity," Duddy whispered.

"That's okay," Charity said in a syrupy voice. "Like I told Todd, Vespa's a little too spiteful for my taste. I prefer to play someone classier, like Varusa, the Lizard Queen. Duddy, would you like to join us?"

Duddy's eyes lit up for a second, but then he cleared his throat. "Uh . . . well, I did promise Lucy that I'd help her. It takes two people to work the lasers and stop the atoms from zipping back and forth." He gave me a sheepish grin.

"Todd, you and I could have a duel by ourselves at your place," Charity suggested.

Lucy whirled back around to the whiteboard, and I stared at the carpet, trying to get my head around Duddy not wanting to come . . . and Charity wanting to play just with me. There was also the small-but-not-really issue of the Toddlians. If Charity came back to my house, what was I supposed to do with them? "Erm, it's getting a little late, and I have some pre-algebra homework . . ."

Duddy shot me a surprised look, and I swear Lucy grinned at her whiteboard. Even Charity seemed confused, then finally said, "Well, this has been stimulating, but I've got to get home and help my mom with dinner."

"Right," I said, feeling kind of relieved. For some reason I was really eager to get out of this room. "I'd better go too."

Charity and I each picked up our things, and after some quick goodbyes, we were headed in opposite directions on the sidewalk—her toward her house, me toward mine.

I chewed my lip as I walked, thinking.

What was going on with my friends?

CHAPTER 11

PERSEPHONE

"**W**here's Herman?" young Marty asked me, sidling up as I brushed Tenderfoot the cricket in her matchstick stall.

"Durned if I know," I said, shaking my head. Herman'd been MIA since the *Exodus* disaster. Lewis'd seen him holed up in his new office, really just a study room off the library, reading printouts from that dadgummed Intra-Net Todd was always going slack-jawed in front of. "Probably molderin' away somewhere, workin' on his 'Big Plan.'"

"Do we know what his New Big Plan is?" Chester wondered. "Since the boat sank?"

"Nope. All's we know is thet he has one. Mebbe he's

planning on settin' up a ranch somewheres." *Hopefully in Lucy's room. Now that is a gal I sure could get used to. She has some get-up-'n'-go.*

Suddenly Marty looked up and then pointed into the air. "Er . . . what's that?"

There was a roar of wings like a locomotive steamin' full blast, the exact same noise we'd heard before.

"L-look!" Chester stammered, pointing into the air. Two ginormous black beasts with bulgy red eyes flew lightnin' fast from the direction of the Red Thing Lucy'd called an "apple." My mouth went dry.

"RUN!" I screamed to Marty, but he didn't move on account of havin' fainted dead away. "Aw, for the love of Pete." I ain't afeared of much, but when I saw those red glittery eyes up close, I threw Marty over my shoulder and lit a shuck for the nearest hut like nobody's business.

As I ran, one of them buzzin' bullies landed in Lake Parkay, rubbin' its nasty, hairy legs together like it was prayin' before eatin' its meal: *us.*

Herman appeared out of nowhere, and he and Lewis yanked us into the Library of Higher Learning and helped me lay the conked-out lad on a toe-hair rug. They were hunkered down inside with Chester, peekin' out the door at the destruction.

"We heard them, too!" Lewis said, shaking so bad I thought he'd scramble his brains. "What are they, Herman?"

"I looked them up in my *Guide to Household Insects*. *Musca domestica*—common houseflies. Foul creatures, depositing disease and feces wherever they land." Herman shuddered. "Will the plagues of the Re—the *apple* never cease?"

"What's 'feces'?" Chester asked.

"No time to jaw," I said. "Unless you found out how to kill the vermin, Herman."

"What we need is a weapon called a 'fly swatter,'" Herman said, giving the room a once-over. "No time to construct one now."

I skedaddled over the desk, where he'd put together a tiny version of a bigger, more elaborate boat than *The Exodus*. "What's this? You hidin' the big boat somewheres? With a long plank, we could skewer those vermin right through the liver . . ."

"Please, Persephone!" Herman yelped. "Do not disassemble my new boat! I've been laboring over it for days, and to have it splattered with . . ." He shuddered again.

"Fly guts?" I finished. "'Cause iffin we don't get out there and stop those brutes, it'll be *our* guts splatterin'."

Lewis looked like he was about to make like Marty and keel over. "Doncha even think about it, Lew," I ordered. "Lookee there! The other one's in the lake now. Boys, they're gonna drain it dry!"

And sure enough, that's what those furry-legged fiends did. Then they flapped like furies, causing a twister that knocked over our rebuilt swing set and nearly flattened every hut on Butroche Boulevard. Thankfully, most of the folk had holed up in the school, even though the school day was long over. Unfortunately, that's where the buzzin' buzzards headed next, and the people let loose with earsplittin' screams.

The smaller fly circled the school's dome, like a hawk sightin' a squeaker. The big one hurled itself at the roof, knockin' the purty cellophane stained glass winder clean out.

"My masterpiece!" Lewis gasped. "That took Daisy and me three days to create! Oh no! It's sticking its head in the hole!"

There were shrieks of "Noooooo!" and "GREAT TODD SAVE US!" risin' up out of the building, while every male in eyesight wrung his hands and sat on his fanny. Just like our god, Todd. Wellsiree, I'd done had it.

"You boys got thirty seconds to come up with a way to kill those flies, or I'm goin' after 'em myself." I picked up Herman's precious boat model to prove I weren't barkin' at the knot this time. "Now where are them wood planks? Put up or shut up, fellas."

"Put *that*"—Herman pointed at the tiny boat—"on my desk and simmer down. I have an idea. In the words of—"

"We don't have time for no highfalutin quote now, Herman. Cain't you hear them screamin'? Now unrip yer plan!"

He flared his nostrils like a spooked horse, and I

knew I'd made him mad. But I didn't have time to pussy-foot around. Finally, he filled his lungs and said, "We have to work as a team . . ."

Turns out Herman's plan was to get our beefiest boys to haul the rank sweat sock Todd had left for us earlier as far from Toddlandia as we could get it. Meanwhile, the rest of us would fill the backsides of those bulgy-eyed bugs with buckshot using slingshots and rocks.

I liked it. Except for the part where I got to play decoy. But, as usual, I was the only one with the gumption to lay my life on the line. I whistled to Tumbleweed, my second favorite cricket after Tenderfoot, who somehow managed to hear me above all the ruckus. She hopped over, and I shimmied up to the library roof and threw myself onto her back as she sailed past. "GERONIMO!" I hollered. "I'm comin' for ya, ya overgrown, uglified insect!"

That got the fly's attention. It whipped its huge head around, flicked its wings twice, and rubbed its hairy legs together.

"You'd *better* say your prayers!" I yelled. "'Cause you done messed with the wrong cowgirl!"

I swung my floss lasso wide and slung it with all my might. It hit its mark and noosed that vermin right around the neck. That critter bucked and kicked and tried to free itself with four of its legs. Its pardner circled Toddlandia, stirring up so much dander and debris we could scarcely see. "Get yerself some rocks from the playground!" I called above the clamor. "Use the rubber bands from the swings and pair up to make catapult thingies." The fly started to lift off, dragging me with it. "Make tracks, tinhorns!"

I was high enough off the ground now to see the sock traveling west across the Fiber Forest like a duck on water.

"Let 'er rip!" I cried to my swing-shot posse, letting go of the lasso.

"For Toddlandia!" Lewis whooped as he ran out of the library, hurling books at the air. Herman crawled out then, too, and commenced to ordering everybody around.

But by that time those demon dive-bombers had their hides so full of rocks from our swing-shots that they zipped out of our neck of the woods and headed straight for the sock.

"I don't reckon they'll be showin' their carcasses around here any time soon," I said to my amigos. "Mighty proud of all y'all!"

There were a few wimpified cheers, but most of the Toddlians jest collapsed where they stood.

One who was still standin' was Little Cynthia, who came up to me and pulled on my chaps fringe. "I'm hungry," she whined. In a minute, everybody else started bellyachin' about there bein' next to nothin' to eat.

Herman climbed to the top of the playground slide.

"My valiant Toddlians, your heroism this day will be recorded in the annals of Toddlian history as a glorious and victorious battle."

"If you keep throwin' away our food, *we'll* be history, and there won't be anybody left alive to write nothin'," I pointed out.

The others mumbled in agreement.

"I admit, my hastily formed plan was flawed." He eyeballed the sock. "Did anyone see from whence the flies flew in? Perhaps we could find a means of blocking their way of entering our territory."

Lewis stood in the center of the teeter-totter, his wobbly knees knockin' like a newborn calf. He pointed, wide-eyed. "They came from . . . the Red Thing!"

The people began bemoanin' their fate, which was lookin' purty grim.

Herman nodded. "Yes, I see that Todd still has not disposed of the offensive object. Friends, I know that we were disappointed in the maiden voyage of *The Exodus . . .*"

"Maiden voyage?" I scoffed. "Maiden voyage to the bottom of the sea, mebbe."

Herman narrowed his eyes at me. "Nevertheless, this attack makes the danger in our situation clear. While that rotten apple remains, it's only a matter of time before this happens again. Toddlandia is under siege. Conditions can only deteriorate as long as we are out of favor with His Toddness. We now have nothing with which to nourish ourselves, no water supply, our huts are in shambles . . . For some reason our god has set his face against us. Which clearly means—"

"That I need to talk to him again!" Lewis said, all desperate-like.

Herman shook his head. "No, my tenderhearted friend. There is no time left for that. As William Mather Lewis said, 'The tragedy of life is not that it ends so soon, but that we wait so long to begin it.' Our days are numbered if we remain any longer here. We must begin life anew. Therefore, all our efforts must be toward my *new* new plan, Operation Anchors Aweigh. Time is of the essence. Let me explain . . ."

I let him explain away and kept to my own counsel. One thing I knew for sure: I was plumb relieved there hadn't been a vote to tally. I'd have felt regretful about saying "nay" to keeping Todd.

But votin' against Lew? That woulda broke my heart right down the middle.

CHAPTER 12

I was swimming in a secluded cove, floating on my back while Charity danced around on the beach in a cheesy bee costume, complete with sparkly pom-pom antennae. She waved to me and laughed, then skipped over to a palm tree, climbed it, and started hurling coconuts at my head.

"Hey! Stop that!" I hollered, sitting up . . . *in my bed?*

It had been a dream, except something *was PING, PING, PING*ing against my window. Somebody was pelting it with pebbles! I shuffled over to the window and looked out.

Lucy?

I rubbed my eyes and strained to see without my

glasses. Lucy waved like she was landing an airplane, motioning for me to come outside. I sighed and slipped on my robe and a pair of super-fuzzy polka-dot slipper socks I'd borrowed from my mom ever since the Toddlians took over my real slippers.

I hugged my robe around me as I walked out into the cool October night. Lucy was standing under the big tree in our backyard, staring up at the starry sky.

"That's Ursa Major," she said, pointing up at the Big Dipper. "The Bear." Lucy looked at me with shiny eyes. "Sorry for waking you, Todd. Thanks for meeting me."

"Sure," I said, still not really sure why I was there.

Lucy took a deep breath and exhaled, making a little cloud. "Oh, cool! Condensation." She flipped her wild, crazy-curly hair over her shoulder. "You know what causes that? It's the carbon dioxide and the moisture from your mouth and lungs. Inside your lungs the molecules can move freely because it's warm, but out here . . ." Lucy shivered and seemed to forget what she was saying.

"But out here?" I repeated.

"Oh, yeah. In order for water to stay in its gas form as a vapor, it requires energy to keep the molecules moving. They lose energy in the cold and have to 'huddle' together—forming a fog, as it were, of tiny droplets."

"Umm . . . did you wake me up to talk about breath clouds?"

Lucy giggled nervously. "No. I'll get to the point. Have you heard of the Fall Ball that the community center's hosting?"

"The big dance? Yeah, but . . ." *Oh, man.* Was she going to ask me to go with her?

She nodded and leaned into my face. "Duddy asked me to go with him after you and Charmaine left."

I was too shocked to correct her. My sleep fog started to lift, and I realized why Duddy had been at Lucy's house this afternoon . . . and why he'd *stayed.* He liked Lucy! Wait—he liked *Lucy*?

She wrapped her arms around herself, still shivering. "It kind of freaked me out. After all, dancing requires close proximity to your partner. Close enough for *philematology.*" She glanced over at me and then quickly looked away.

"Fill-a-whatta?"

"You know, the anatomical juxtaposition of two *orbicularis oris* muscles in a state of contracting."

"Huh?"

Lucy pointed to her lips and leaned toward me. "*Kissing!* Don't you think we're too young to exchange saliva and all that gross stuff? Shouldn't we save that kind of contact until we've at least cleared puberty by a few years?"

I took a step back. The thought of my two best friends smooching made me feel all wiggly and gross, like touching a slug. *Ew!* And besides, that would ruin everything! Couldn't Duddy see that?

Lucy closed the distance between us. "Anyway, aren't dances just vestiges of a materialistic Disney Channel lifestyle that promotes the Puberty-Is-One-Big-Party-Just-Believe-In-Yourself-and-Boogie-the-Night-Away tripe they feed the tween crowd? Isn't all this musical pairing up and happily-ever-aftering really a big ruse to promote fifties-era femininity and sell makeup? It's all about commercialism, conformity to the Ken-and-Barbie culture, and preserving the archaic idea of a patriarchal society, I mean . . ." She looked up at me. Her face was red. She took a deep breath. *"Don't you think?"*

Wow. She was worked up. "Erm . . . I didn't really get much of that." I tried to change the subject. "Wait, you don't like the Disney Channel? Because I think *Phineas and Ferb* is pretty funny."

Lucy sighed the way she does when she gives me her *you cretin!* look. But instead she sat on the bench under the tree and patted it for me to join her. The stone was cold, and I wrapped my robe tighter around me.

"Cute slipper socks," she said. "Are those Totes Toasties? My grandma has a pair of those."

I suddenly regretted my fashion decision. "Um, I don't know. My mom got them. They keep my feet warm."

"Speaking of warming things up, Todd, don't you

think that kids our age are too young for the whole dating scene?" She was staring me right in the eye.

Was she right? Were we too young to date? Well, I'd walked home with Charity, and we *had* been going to get dressed up and role-play together . . .

I shrugged. "I dunno. I feel like maybe we're old enough to date. You know, if we find the right person." I stood, eager to get back to my room and away from this conversation.

But when I turned back, I saw that Lucy had dropped her eyes and was sighing again. I almost felt bad.

"Look, I'm just tired, and I don't really know what you want me to tell you."

Her hair hid most of her face as she bent her head toward mine. "Tell me whether or not I should say yes."

What was I supposed to say? Duddy must've been pretty gaga for her to skip playing *Dragon Sensei* and listen to all her atomic gibberish. It was a no-brainer what he'd want me to do, and after all, he was my best friend. "Sure. Duddy's a great guy. Tell him you'll go with him."

"Oh," Lucy said in a tiny voice. She shook her hair out of her face and stared at her folded hands. I was getting the sense that I'd said totally the wrong thing. Again.

I stood up and stretched. "Well, listen, I'm going back to bed. It's really late, you know, and public school starts early . . ." She didn't respond or even look up at me.

"Good night, Lucy," I said softer, and then I reached out and patted her slumped shoulder. She looked up at me in surprise. I was kind of surprised too.

Why did I do that? I didn't waste any more time in turning around and shuffling back inside.

CHAPTER 13

When I walked up to the school steps the next morning, Duddy gave me a huge bear hug. I peeled him off me and looked around to make sure nobody'd seen us. "Dude, what are you thinking?"

"I'm sorry," he said, grinning like a maniac. "But I have the *best* news! You'll never guess."

"Lucy said yes." I thought that might simmer him down, but I thought wrong.

"Yesssss!" he said with a flying fist pump. "She texted me this morning and said she'd be deeeelighted to go with me to the Fall Ball!" He stopped celebrating long enough to wonder: "Hey! How'd you know that? Who told you I'd asked her?"

"Really, Dud? You'd rather build some hi-tech clock than play *Dragon Sensei*?" I tapped my temple. "It's not rocket science."

He giggled and blushed. "Even Ike and Wendell have dates! They asked a couple of girls on their Odyssey of the Minds team. I guess they got to know them building some kind of underwater colony using pop bottles. Cool, huh?"

Ike and Wendell have dates too? It was an epidemic! What was happening to all my friends?

Then I spotted a gorgeous girl giving us the Saki Salute across the courtyard. *Charity.* What was happening to *me*?

We saluted back as she approached. "You should totally ask her to the dance, Todd," Duddy whispered. "I bet she's dying for you to!"

I didn't answer him. Watching Charity walk toward me, her hair glistening in the early morning sunlight, her smile just for me, I tried to imagine what it'd be like to dance with her to a slow song. Suddenly my throat felt all tight, and I started to sweat.

Then there was my little chat with Lucy last night, when she told me she thought dances were dumb. Was she right? I wasn't sure, but something about what she'd said had me feeling weird about asking Charity to the Fall Ball.

The thing is, if dances were so dumb, why was Lucy going?

"Well, this is it," I said to Duddy, as we parted ways in the hall. I was headed to music (Charity's idea; she was taking it, too) since being on the swim team got me out of gym and added a new elective to my schedule. "Think you can handle being on your own?"

Duddy shrugged. "Sure! I'm not worried." That was good, because I was worried enough for the both of us. "Besides, Ernie will be my bodyguard, won't you, Ernie?"

Ernie was waiting by the door to escort Duddy into gym class. Since it seemed *Catttthhaaaaandra* hadn't succeeded in getting them on the badminton team yet, he'd been added to our old gym class. "Of courth!" he said around his retainer. "Thath what friendth are for! Thothe guyth won't meth with Duddy, I thwear it." He held his hand out to me, and I shook it.

If you'd had told me a few weeks ago that our former elementary school tormentor, Ernie "Swirly Lord" Buchenwald, would be pledging to *protect* Duddy, I'd have said you were certifiable. But middle school is a strange place.

As if to prove that true, a giant girl with frizzy, flaming red hair came barreling around the corner and bulldozed into Ernie . . . on purpose. He belly-flopped onto the floor.

Normally I would have expected him to jump up and pummel her. Instead, Ernie stood, wheezing like he was having a coronary. He was laughing that hard. Reaching up, he pulled her down into a headlock.

"Thith afternoon, lother! YOU. ME," she said, and then nodded at Duddy. "Dragon Mathter here. BADMINTON! HAW HAW!"

The girl wrestled free from Ernie's grip and picked him up from behind like he was a little kid. She had to have been six feet tall, with the shoulders of a line-backer. But the biggest thing about her was her retainer. It made Ernie's look minuscule.

She swung him around in a circle a couple of times. He laughed so hard his retainer shot out and hit the gym-door glass, leaving a big spitty spot. Then she dropped him and lumbered off toward the seventh grade hall. "LATER, LOTHERTH!"

"That was Cassandra," Ernie said, as if there was any confusion. He stared dreamily after her as he picked his retainer up.

"You know, Ernie's new friend," Duddy explained, wiggling his eyebrows.

Ernie sighed. He wiped his retainer on his sleeve and popped it back into his mouth, still staring down the seventh grade hall. "And perhapth thomething more."

He turned to us with a goofy metal grin. "You thould thee her hit a thuttlecock. Thee can really thlam that thucker!" He wiped the drool from his mouth with the back of his hand. "I don't know what it ith about her . . . thee'th jutht tho *bewitching.*"

Duddy rolled his eyes, and I bit my cheek to keep from laughing.

"So, Ernie," I said casually, "are you taking your badminton babe to the dance?"

"Oh," Ernie said, drooling, "I can only hope. Tho far I haven't got up the guth to athk her."

The warning bell rang, and Duddy and Ernie walked into gym without me.

I looked at Charity and smiled. But as we turned around and strolled toward the music room, part of me really wished I was heading into the gym with Ernie and Duddy.

Afternoon announcements notified the WAVES that we were back in the water after school. Practice was back on, and I was looking forward to improving my strokes minus Max. I walked out of the dressing room and joined the other swimmers, who were splashing around in the shallow end. A shrill whistle split the air, and everybody froze. We all looked toward the sound, and a collective shudder ran through the pool.

Instead of nice but slightly neurotic Madame Dauphinee, *Terrifying Coach Tomlin* descended the bleachers. He marched over to us, whistle between his teeth.

My heart stopped. *What's he doing here?* I looked around at my fellow WAVES. Everyone looked as confused as I was.

"All right, you water lilies!" Coach Tomlin bellowed. "Your days of wine, roses, and crêpes are OVER! Madame Dauphinee has taken a leave of absence. Starting now, I'm your new swim coach, and I'm going to make real athletes out of you wet sandwiches!"

What was he talking about? Was Madame Dauphinee out for good?

A simultaneous moan rose up from the older kids. Even us sixth graders had heard the horror stories: running endless suicides; impossible obstacle courses, complete with punji sticks and slime pits; and his infamous "chuck-ups," which were piggyback push-ups for being late. (Apparently doing fifty push-ups with a passenger pretty much guaranteed you would upchuck.)

Coach Tomlin blew another ear-splitting whistle. "Get your keisters out of that pool and line up. Pronto!" We pulled ourselves out of the water and lined up, but it wasn't fast enough for The Ogre. "Move it! Move it! Move it!"

Once we were ready for inspection, he crossed his arms and looked us over. I'd never seen him up close, but the man was built like a tank. For a guy his age, he was amazingly ripped. I felt like a teeny, helpless little Toddlian as he studied me. It actually made me wonder how I looked to them. He shook his head, then moved his glare down the line.

When he'd finished "inspecting" the team, Blaine Simons, a skinny eighth grade boy with white-blond hair, spoke up: "Uh, when is Madame Dauphinee coming back?"

Coach Tomlin turned to him with a laser-like glare. "What, am I not good enough for you?"

Blaine sputtered. "No, it's just—just—"

"JUST WHAT?" Coach Tomlin thundered. "You think I don't have anything better to do than babysit a bunch of gym-shy tadpoles? Miss Dauphinee isn't coming back from Provence till next year at the earliest. I've gone out of my way to adjust my schedule to whip you limp pollywogs into shape. THANK ME."

The "initiated" older kids shouted, "THANK YOU, SIR!" and the rest of us caught on quick.

"WHAT WAS THAT?"

"THANK YOU, SIR!" everybody screamed.

Coach Tomlin gave us a curt nod. "That's better. Now"—he went down the line, poking his stubby finger into faces—"you, you, you, you, and"—he got to me and smushed his finger into my nose—"*you*, get in the water and show me what you're made of. NOW!"

"Thank you, sir!" I squeaked along with the other victims.

"Kick it!" Coach Tomlin called once we were in our lanes. "Show me your kicking action!"

I kicked as if my life depended on it. For all I knew, it might.

Coach bent over the edge with his mouth in my ear. "That all you got, swimmer? How'd you make it on this team with those weak legs? I could snap you like a toothpick!" No matter how hard we kicked, he insisted we were slacking.

And for some reason, he seemed to especially have it in for *me*. "Iron Lung!" he barked. "Swim as long as you can, NO breath. Let's separate the men from the boys!" I took the biggest breath I could and dove under the water. By halfway down the second lap my lungs were on fire and my head was about to explode. I managed to make it all the way to the edge, though, before I shot out of the water, gasping. Maybe all of those swirlies had conditioned me, but I made it longer than anyone else.

"What's your name, swimmer?" he demanded. Whatever I panted must've sounded to him like "Buttrock," Max's charming nickname for me, because that's what he decided to call me. "All right, everybody out but Buttrock here." The other five WAVES hoisted themselves, heaving, out of the pool. They looked as relieved as lobsters who'd escaped the pot. And what did that make me?

I was too exhausted to even be scared. But I did hope he wouldn't humiliate me in front of Charity. Swimming was my one skill. "Dead-man drag!" he announced, crossing his arms.

That did not sound good. "You there!" He picked out the biggest eighth grade guy and made him get in the water with me, clasping my ankles. "Now down and back, Buttrock, fast as you can. NO kicking, dead man. Make him work his upper body."

Whoever said water made you weightless was outta their mind. I was pretty sure I'd shredded every muscle in my arms and torso by the time I hauled that kid to the wall and back. My back burned, my arms burned, my abs felt like flaming fireplace pokers were running up and down them. I finally reached the wall and shook that guy off me.

"Hmmm," Coach Tomlin growled. "Better than I thought you'd do, but you're still not living up to your full potential. You have to *want it*! You're gonna thank me for this. Get out!"

"Thank you, sir," I breathed, dragging my quivering body from the pool. He told us to line up again. Charity came and stood next to me, giving my hand a quick squeeze when Coach Tomlin wasn't looking. That put a little spark back into me.

"Listen up, swimmers. That pitiful display of unpre-
paredness I just witnessed proves that you are unworthy
of water. The pool is for closers! No one gets back in
the water until you have strong quads, pecs, glutes . . ."
Tomlin flexed each muscle group as he spoke. "And most
of all, you have to prove to me that you have *heart*!" He
slammed his fist against his chest hard enough to break
an average breastbone, and looked at me. "You have
to want to win more than you want your next breath.
You're gonna thank me for kicking your keisters when
we bring home that team trophy."

"Thank you, sir," Blaine blurted by himself.

Coach Tomlin flicked a glance at him and muttered,
"No one likes a suck-up, kid." Then he pointed to the
locker rooms. "Now go get rid of those ridiculous swim-
suits. You have exactly two minutes point seven seconds
to meet me back here in your sneakers. Go!"

Everyone gawped at each other in confusion. He
wanted us to do *what*? Blaine raised his hand and
asked, "Do you want us to wear anything besides our
sneakers?"

The coach rubbed his buzz and blinked at Blaine.
"Are you sassing me, boy? Because I'd hate to have to
hang you by your toes off the high dive."

"N-n-no, s-s-sir," Blaine said, backing toward the
locker room.

"Good," Coach Tomlin boomed. "Sassypants here
has just cost you all thirteen seconds." He clicked his

stopwatch. "You now have exactly one minute fifty-four seconds to meet me back here. Extra chuck-ups to whoever's late! Now go!"

"THANK YOU, SIR!" we screamed as we scrambled to the locker rooms.

Clothes flew in all directions as we raced against the clock. One of the older guys urged us to hurry. He'd evidently once paid the piggyback push-up price for being late once. "The golden age of WAVES is over, boys," he sighed, shoving his T-shirt over his head. I had no idea what that meant, but I mentally kissed those crêpes goodbye.

As I went to pull on my pants I realized I'd put my tighty-whities on inside out *and* backward. There was no time to fix the situation. I just prayed Coach Tomlin didn't have some kind of wedgie torture in his arsenal of cruel and unusual punishment.

By some miracle we all managed to make it back in line before time was up. Tomlin marched us all into the weight room, where we were saddled with ten-pound dumbbells.

"Your objective is to run circles around the pool until I tell you otherwise," Coach Tomlin said. He deafened us with the whistle and roared, "RUN! KNEES UP! GO! GO! GO!"

We ran. After three laps, I had a massive side stitch that doubled me over. Suddenly an icy blast of water hammered me in the temple. I yelped and turned toward

Tomlin, who was aiming the hose right at me. "This ought to cool you off, hot stuff! Now RUN! Thank me."

"THANK YOU, SIR," I yelled through gritted teeth. Where did this guy get off treating us like we were in boot camp? Summoning all my strength, I hefted the dumbbells onto my hips and started jogging again.

Behind me, I heard some smart-alecky seventh grader whispering that the huge laminated signs on the walls clearly stated, "absolutely no running allowed."

"I MAKE THE RULES NOW, SASSYPANTS!" came Coach Tomlin's reply.

As I rounded the far end of the pool I watched the poor dude get hosed at close range. The coach motioned to me. "Buttrock, come help Mr. Sassypants here learn a little lesson."

I jogged over on jiggly legs. Coach ripped the weights out of my cramped hands. "Since Mr. Sassypants here has issues with running around the pool, we're gonna let him run up and down these bleacher steps . . . with *you* on his back. Thank me."

We thanked him. The kid looked at me with fear in his eyes. Fortunately, Tomlin had stomped over to terrorize someone else with the hose and missed it. The seventh grader was skinnier than me and looked like a strong wind would carry him away. How he was going to hold my weight and keep his balance was beyond me.

"Are you ready?" I asked once he'd bent over. He nodded, and I hopped onto his wet, bony back, looping my arms through his. We trotted up and down the stairs, and I wished with everything in me that I'd taken two extra seconds and turned my underwear around right.

We ran stairs until my human horse was wheezing so bad I knew we were going to both bash our brains out on the bleachers.

Coach Tomlin must've been thinking the same thing, because he whistled us down and hosed us off. The seventh grader collapsed into a little ball at his feet, and Tomlin decided that this was the time to officially call it quits. He blew his stupid whistle, lined us up, and told everybody to go home and "drink protein shakes. Especially Mr. Sassypants."

I glanced down the lineup at Charity. She was sweaty and breathing hard but didn't look damaged. Maybe she wouldn't be too disappointed about not having me to hang with in music class or swim practice. Nothing Max could do to me in gym could compare to the brutal humiliation of The Ogre. I staggered into the locker room and changed with shaking hands, then hustled out to find Charity, who was waiting by the exit.

The coach was winding the hose around his arm as I skittered past. I could feel his steely eyes follow me as I talked to Charity. "Let's get out of here," I said, leading the way out of the pool building. "You okay?"

She flashed the dimpled grin that gave me goose bumps. "Yeah. That was intense, though. Coach Tomlin sure seemed to like you."

Like me? Girls were so hard to read. I snorted. "If he liked me any more he'd have killed me. I'm ready to quit the swim team. Aren't you?"

Charity sat on the bench under the big tree and played with her ponytail. "Oh, I'm not sure. It was definitely challenging, and Coach T is a little rough."

"You *think*?"

"But I can see where he's coming from, you know? We really have no business swimming until we've built up the stamina and muscle strength to go the distance. In the end, I think it's going to help us be better swimmers. Wouldn't that be cool?"

Cool was the very last thing I thought *any* of this was! "You . . . really think he knows what he's doing?"

"Did you see his muscles? His legs looked like Sensei Nagee's! Maybe we should trust him, Todd."

I didn't know what to say. I didn't think I'd make it through another warm-up with Terrifying Coach Tomlin, much less an entire practice. I didn't want to seem like a total wimp and quit, and I'd hate to give up spending Max-free time with Charity, but there was only so much a guy could take. *"You're not living up to your potential!"* echoed in my ears.

"You want to come to my house and hang out? I've got the new Varusa action figure doll. She came with her own Fernsopian pool!"

I'd had enough pools, but I might not get the chance

to hang with Charity after I quit the swim team. She smiled wider, and I almost said yes. But I was probably more exhausted than I'd ever been in my entire life, and as much as I wanted to spend more time with her, I knew I just needed to go home, lie down in my room, and rest my already aching muscles. *And feed the Toddlians.* It would be responsible to actually take care of them for once, but also, I couldn't deny, I could kind of use a couple of hours with a bunch of people who worshipped me.

"Not today," I said, giving her the best smile I could muster. "I'm pretty tired."

She looked disappointed for a second, but her smile came back. "Seeya, then!" She nodded and left.

I hurried home to see my little people, who at least thought I was all-powerful and full of awesomeness. Sometimes it felt good to be a god.

CHAPTER 14

LEWIS

I paced back and forth on a frond of a Fernsopian fern, staring at Saki as she hurled a screaming Boom Shroom across Todd's *Dragon Sensei* bedspread. There was a time when I hadn't appreciated the glaring colors of this comforter, but now they were dear to me. Here, I had talked with Great Todd about his hopes, fears, and dreams.

Was all that behind us now? Or could I convince my god to accept my people back into his good graces? If he persisted in rejecting us, the others would certainly vote to sail Herman's repaired vessel into the vast unknown, searching for another divine leader.

I sighed and checked the digital clock on Todd's desk: 4:37. Surely he would be home soon, and then our fate would be decided.

With a heavy heart I climbed upon the pillow. It contained a veritable feast of tasty Todd dirt for me to enjoy, but how could anyone eat in the depths of despair? Besides, my appetite had not returned since the unfortunate voyage of *The Exodus*.

I tried to picture my life without Todd to guide me, but I could not. I *was* Todd; from him I had sprung. There was no one else I wanted to worship with my unfailing friendship and devotion.

"Lewis," I said to myself. "You *must* believe. Believe in your ability to convince Todd to summon that caring, loving god he once was and, deep within, still is!"

I forced myself to eat a few dandruff flakes so that I would have the strength I needed for the trial ahead. I scarcely tasted the crispy, delectable dead skin, so overwhelmed was my mind with what I wanted to say. Perhaps I should have accepted Persephone's offer to help me create cue cards . . .

No! This time I had to speak straight from the heart.

At last Todd's door swung open, and His Greatness trudged to his desk and dropped his backpack on it. He walked to the bed and nearly sat his posterior on my person. "Oh, Todd live forever, WAIT!" I screamed, diving out from under him just in time. "I beg a word with your worship!"

"Lewis?" Todd said, grabbing his micro-glasses from the desk and leaning over me. From the way his eyebrows arched, I assumed he was surprised to see me.

"What are you doing here? Why aren't you in Toddlandia with everybody else?"

I cleared my throat and tried to still my trembling voice. "Erm . . . could we *talk*?"

He shrugged, which I interpreted as a yes. I started to climb up his arm, as was our custom, but he plucked me from his sleeve and set me on the pillow. "I can see you better this way," he explained. "What's up?"

I paced back and forth on the pillow, trying to keep the words from tumbling out all at once. "I am not sure if I have ever expressed to you, Great One, just how much your friendship means to me." I turned to face him and took a deep breath. "Being the Toddlian who is especially close to you is more important to me than I can express—"

The doorbell rang, and Todd jumped off the bed, threw off his glasses, and raced out of his room. He came back a moment later, put the glasses back on, and flopped down, bouncing me off balance.

"Uh . . . sorry," he said. "I just thought that might be . . . *someone*."

"Someone important?" I asked.

"Yeah. But it was just one of Mom's little-kid piano students." Todd yawned. "What were you saying?"

I couldn't risk another interference; I cleared my throat and said quickly, "Lately my people and I can't help feeling that we have lost your favor."

"I don't know what you mean by that," he said with a frown.

Not a good beginning, Lewis. I swallowed and looked down at my feet. "We feel that you are no longer pleased with us."

"What makes you think that?"

Take courage, Lewis, it's now or never. "Ahem, well . . . there was the rotten Red Thing—the apple you left by your Refuse Dome. It grew a terrifying worm and then bore two fearsome winged creatures that reeked chaos on Toddlandia." I shuddered at the memory. "The destruction was extensive; have you not noticed the damage done to our community center roof and the collapse of several huts? But the emotional toll was the heaviest upon us, especially since we believe it to be some sort of sign from you . . ."

Todd rubbed his hands through his hair in an agitated manner. "Crud, no, I hadn't noticed. Look, I'm sorry. You just can't imagine the stress I'm under trying to keep track of all of you, trying to keep from getting killed by Max, trying to keep *you* from getting killed by Max . . . and now I've got The Ogre on my case . . . it's just a lot, okay?"

He punched the bed, nearly knocking me over again. I steadied myself and walked to the edge of the pillow, looking up into his micro-glasses. I wasn't sure what an ogre was, but I knew the terrors of Max firsthand. *Poor Todd.*

"Would you like to talk about it, Great One?"

He sighed. "It wouldn't do any good."

"We were confidants once . . . compadres, I thought. Could we just . . . go back to the way it used to be? The way *you* used to be?" I lifted my blurry eyes to his and said with all my soul, "Please?"

Todd peeled off the glasses and tossed them aside. "I'm not a good god now, is that what you're saying?" He studied the ceiling. "I give you dirty clothes to eat, I hide you from Max. I change your water, most of the time . . ." He looked at me then. "Remember, I told you in the beginning I wasn't good at this sort of thing!" Todd threw in his hands in the air and sunk onto the bed. "I just don't know what else you want from me."

I tried not to sound as desperate as I felt. "We only want your guidance and . . . friendship."

"OK, then," he said glumly. "I'll try to live up to my *full potential.* How about that?" He stood, pulled off the glasses, and plodded to his desk, where he threw them down. "Sorry, Lewis. It's just that I've got stuff to do."

Todd plopped into his desk chair. He opened his laptop and plugged in his headphones, cutting off all communication.

I slid off the pillow and lay prostrate on the bed, too

soul-weary to move. I don't know how long I had lain there when the doorbell rang again. And rang. And rang.

Finally Todd groaned, flung his headphones onto his desk, and yelled to no one in particular, "DON'T WORRY, I'LL GET IT!" He stomped out of the room, slamming the door with terrific force.

The tears that had been begging to be released now threatened to spill out, and I blinked to stop myself from having what Persephone called a "sissified fit." As if I had summoned her, Persephone appeared from under Todd's pillow. She had been there, silently supporting me, all along.

It was nice to have a true friend.

Persephone walked over and patted my back. "I could jest drag that Todd through a cactus patch for treatin' you like this, Lew. You deserve better. All of us do."

I could not answer her. My voice was being choked by the grief of losing my god . . . my friend.

"I reckon this is it, then—I'll tell Herman and the others to commence packin'. I know this is hard for you, bein' Todd's partic'lar friend and all." Her eyes shone, and her voice swelled with excitement. "But just think, Lew! We'll ride the waves aboard *The Exodus* into the wild blue yonder and a brand-new life!"

A whimper escaped me, and I ran away from Persephone. The sissified fit had come.

CHAPTER 15

"**S**top ringing the stupid doorbell already," I muttered, opening the door to see what the emergency was.

"Why hello, Little Butty!"

Max? Seriously? Could this day possibly get any worse? He advanced toward me.

"Sorry, Max. You must have gotten the day wrong." I started slowly closing the door. "Remember, you already had your piano lesson this week, on Wednesday." I'd hoped by some miracle I was right and he was just confused. But I forgot that some unseen force had declared it national "Terrorize Todd Day."

Max used his massive arm to hold the door open. "Oh, I'm not confused. I know exactly what I'm doing."

He pushed past me and strolled into the kitchen, cramming his hand into the jack-o'-lantern candy jar Mom kept on the bar for her students. "It's like this," he said, ripping open a Snickers package with his teeth. "Somehow my parents found out I got kicked off the swim team because of that stupid misunderstanding." He shoved the candy into his mouth and kept talking. "So now I'm back to being short on extracurriculars. I decided to double up on piano lessons and become one of those protégés that plays in Carnegie Hall by the time they're thirteen or whatever. That would show my parents!"

One of Daisy's sippy cups was sitting on the counter. Max picked it up, popped off the lid, and began guzzling what looked like milk.

"Uh, Max. That's—"

"Gah!" he said, spitting Snickers all over me before I could tell him that he'd been drinking toddler formula. "Why'd you let me drink that, man?" he yelled, wiping his mouth off.

It must not have tasted that terrible because pretty soon he was back to describing his great plan. "Anyways, your mom says I play with a lot of 'intensity,' whatever that means, and it might be fun to dress all spiffy and show off my skills in front of thousands of people. And hey, free trip to the Big Apple—give me a chance to try these Cronut things I keep hearing about."

I was barely paying attention to him by then; I was already wondering if Lucy was home, and whether she'd be willing to Toddlian-sit for another night. "Cronuts?" I repeated dumbly, trying to stall him, but suddenly Mom appeared out of nowhere, looking flushed and shoving her frizzy bangs behind her ear.

"Sorry to keep you waiting, Max," she said with a tight smile. "I was on the phone." Here she looked at me with a kind of wild desperation. "That was Mavis from Daisy's playgroup. Apparently your sister's going through a 'biting phase.'" She let out a joyless cackle and led Max into the living room.

Sometimes I worried about the woman.

But right now I had to worry about myself. And the Toddlians, who seemed to think I didn't care about them anymore. Before Max had followed Mom he'd been sure to let me know he wanted to "play with my cool tiny toy collection" later.

I rushed back to my room to collect those "cool tiny toys" and save them from death by magnifying glass or whatever medieval torment Max could think up. I threw on the micro-glasses, grabbed the shoebox from beside my bed, and checked the closet, where they were all dismantling some weird ship thing. Were those my Red Sox cards on the roof?

No time to freak out about that. I had a much bigger freak-worthy problem. "Are you all here?" I asked the Toddlians. "Did Lewis make it back?"

Persephone stopped pulling apart a wad of pink stuff and yelled up to me. "He's safe, no thanks to you! Cain't you see we're plumb up to our eyeballs in repairs here?"

I ignored her rudeness and told them to all stop what they were doing and get back in the shoebox. "Max will be here in a few minutes; can't you hear him?" He was banging out "Frère Jacques" downstairs, missing half the notes. "I gotta get you out of here."

That was all it took. They scurried into the box, some of them muttering about how excited they were to see Lucy again. But, I realized suddenly, I wasn't so sure that *I* wanted to see her. After last night's bizarre talk in the backyard, maybe some distance would be . . . good.

But who else could take them? Duddy was out, because he was off playing badminton with Ernie and Cassandra. And no one else knew about the Toddlians. No one I'd trust with them, anyway.

Max moved on to butchering some scale. I had to do something—fast. "Do we have everybody?" I asked.

"All present and accounted for," Herman replied. "We're eager to have another seminar with Lucy, Your Greatness."

Whatever. I didn't correct him as I closed the lid, then headed into the hallway and shot across to Daisy's room. She was actually asleep in her crib for once, which was amazing considering how loud Max was.

I stopped midstride. What on earth was drawn on her wall? Were those *my* permanent markers all over her floor? *Okay, Todd, deal with it later . . . one crisis at a time.*

I opened Daisy's closet door and hid the Toddlians behind a box of diapers. "I'll get you later," I whispered. I thought I heard a few shouts of dismay as I clicked the door closed, but what could I do?

I ran back into my room and looked around. I needed to find something to use as a decoy to fool Max into believing he actually had the Toddlians. I searched in the closet for an idea . . . *hmmm, better than nothing.*

I grabbed some red Monopoly houses out of the game box and pulled out the rankest, crustiest sock from my laundry hamper. Maybe some of Mom's craziness had spewed onto me, because as I laid the sock on the closet floor I muttered, "Here ya go, Uncle Maxie. Some tiny Toddlians for you to play with." I sprinkled the red houses onto the sock and arranged them neatly into cul-de-sacs. "New Toddlandia needs a hotel or two." I placed two green hotels at opposite ends of the sock. "Have fun with your toys, Max!" Yep, the strain of the day had finally got me.

I found a dirty towel wadded up by my trash can and picked it up. A hideous sick-sweet vinegary stench rose up from a rotten apple. I held my nose and pinched it by its fuzzy stem, then dropped it into the trash with a shudder. The thing was crawling with maggots.

So that's what Lewis was all freaked about. A

harmless apple. I laid the towel carefully over the sock. It was a pretty crude decoy, but then, who was cruder than Max?

The child "protégé's" grand finale was a rousing rendition of "The Farmer in the Dell" (at least I think that's what it was; his "playing" sounded like someone beating the keys with a baseball bat). I sat at my desk and tried to look casual, but there wasn't a muscle in my body that wasn't in a triple-tight knot. Sure enough, within seconds of his last "song," Max burst into my room.

"Done already?" I squeaked out.

"Where are they?" Max growled, slamming the door behind him.

"They're, uh . . . they're not here." I stood in front of the desk like I was protecting it.

He snorted and shoved me out of the way. I landed on my bed and watched him paw through my desk drawers. "So who has them if they aren't here, your *girlfriend*?"

"Please don't—" I said, reaching toward my art drawer as he yanked it out of the desk, turned it over, and dumped it out. Several of my acrylic paints popped open and began oozing onto the carpet. That put enough fire in my belly for me to foolishly say, "And Charity's not my girlfriend."

"I never said anything *about* Charity," Max said with an evil smirk. "You're the one who brought her up." Max was holding my laptop at eye level. He pulled his hands away and let it fall. I lunged and caught it . . . along with his foot in my mouth. I tasted blood and rolled over so he'd think I was more hurt than I was and leave me alone. Plus I didn't want him to see me cry.

"That's nothing compared to what I'm going to do to those little freaks when I'm done with them," he promised as he dug through my dresser drawers. Underwear and socks flew in every direction as he emptied the bottom drawer where I'd hid the Toddlians last time. "I'm gonna stick 'em in the microwave until they pop!" He spread his fingers, presumably to illustrate said Toddlians bursting over the inside surfaces of the appliance. "Nooooo, don't hurt us, Mighty Max," he squealed in a tiny, high voice. "Great Todd, save us! Waaaaahhhh!" Max waved his arms and made a terrified face before busting up at his sadistic self.

He picked up a scrap of paper off the dresser and read it. "What's this? Charity Driscoll's phone number?"

Actually, it was my confirmation code for ordering the new *Dragon Sensei* best-of DVD, but Max didn't give me time to explain.

In two seconds I was off the floor, being held up by the shirt collar till we were nose to nose. "You called her yet, Buttrock? Does she come over here and play with your dumb lizard dolls, or do you two have *better* things to do?" He made smoochy kissing noises, and I shoved away from him, falling back onto the bed. "Maybe we should call her now, so she can hear her dragon warrior scream as I decapitate his little friends."

"That's enough, Max!" I said in a surprisingly brave voice. "Leave Charity out of this."

Max ignored me and threw open the closet door. "Well, well, well. What have we here? A whole little buggy city!"

I squeezed in front of him. "You seriously think I would keep my prize possessions in my filthy closet? Like I told you, they aren't even here."

Max's eyes narrowed, and a slow, evil smile spread across his face. He put his hands under my armpits and tossed me onto the bed. My plan was working! I realized it had a flaw, though. If Max didn't find the sock right away, he'd tear apart what was left of Toddlandia looking for its inhabitants. They didn't deserve that, after all the hours of hard work they'd put into building it.

I crawled between Max's legs and reached for the towel. He took my hint and pulled it off the sock, which was my cue to do a little acting.

"No! Max, please just leave them be. They never did anything to you!"

Max yanked the sock off the floor, and all the Monopoly pieces pelted me. "They're MINE!" he roared, stepping on my head with one boot. "You buggy-wuggies are getting me my A at last, and then it's barbecue time!

What do you think, Todd—Kansas City style, or straight-up Memphis?" He threw back his head and laughed.

I rolled out from under his foot and got on my knees. It was time to dial up the drama. *"No! You can't take them away from meeee!"* I begged and bargained for all I was worth. "I'll do your homework forever, just give them back. Please don't swing them around like that!" Max swung the sock around his head like he was about to throw a lasso and did an awkward victory dance.

And now for the Oscar-winning moment: "I'll teach you everything I know about *Dragon Sensei* so you can impress Charity—" Wait. Did I want to give him that idea?

Lucky for me Max was too busy laughing maniacally to hear what I'd said. "MINE!!!" he boomed, before strutting out the door with his sock.

I sat up, watching him go with a satisfied feeling.

I could only hope he'd get all the way home before realizing the sock was empty.

CHAPTER 16

I got up off my knees and took a deep breath. For once in my life I'd outsmarted somebody without anyone else's input. Okay, so Max wasn't an Einstein or anything, but he'd bought my Toddlian tearjerker act in a way that made me wonder if I might actually be all-powerful.

I checked my face in the mirror on the inside of my closet door. My lip was kind of swollen on one corner, and a stream of blood trickled from where Max's boot had made contact. I grabbed the dirty decoy towel and wiped the blood away. "Butroche," I said to myself in the mirror, "you should go out for the spring musical."

I combed my hair with my fingers and did my best

hot-actor grin, pretending I was on the red carpet, posing for the cameras.

Thinking about cameras reminded me of Lucy's offer to watch the Toddlians for me via webcam. Maybe they could use the protection now. What if Max came over for a piano lesson while I was at swim practice? Or what if he just randomly showed up "to play"? Mom wouldn't know better than to let him in my room.

For that matter, what if Daisy discovered the Toddlians? There was no telling what she might do to the little guys. I'd once seen her bite a beetle in two without blinking an eye.

Wait a second! *The Toddlians!* They were still holed up in Daisy's dark closet. I started toward her room when the doorbell rang again.

My gut twisted, and I froze. Had Max already figured out I'd duped him? Mom must've answered the door, because the bell only rang once. I could hear her talking to someone. Someone who definitely wasn't Max.

Charity. I walked up to the front door just behind Mom and waved. My awful day might actually be turning around!

Charity met my eyes, giving me a hint of a smile, but continued talking to Mom as if I wasn't there. "I don't know what I would have done without Todd, Mrs. Butroche. I'm new to Wakefield, and he's been so sweet to help me feel welcome!" She turned on the dimples, and I thought she was the cutest thing I'd ever seen. Even cuter than VanderPuff as a puppy (before she turned evil).

The beast herself ran in from the living room then, giving Charity's legs a good sniff. "Oh! What a precious little poodle!" Charity crooned as she knelt down and patted the dog. "I just love animals!" From the way VanderPuff was licking Charity's cheek, the feeling was mutual.

Wow. Charity'd even charmed Fluffenstein. I couldn't believe it. That dog hated everybody but Mom.

Charity giggled, then stood and looked at me. "Hi, Todd!" she finally exclaimed.

I blushed and squeaked, "Hi."

Mom whirled around and grabbed my hand. "Here he is!" she sang, pulling me toward Charity. I felt like a complete idiot, especially when Mom wiggled her eyebrows and gave me her *Oooo, it's a girl* googly eyes.

Mom offered Charity some Oreos and milk, but Charity had other ideas. "Actually, Mrs. Butroche," she said, "I stopped by to see if to Todd wants to go for a walk. I just can't get enough of these Boston trees!"

"Umm . . ." I hesitated. Going with Charity meant that it'd be a while before I could rescue the Toddlians from Daisy's closet.

"You do want to come, right, Todd?" Charity added, her voice rising.

"I . . ." Daisy *was* actually sleeping, for once—they'd probably be fine. "Sure," I concluded. I would just have to check on the little guys the second I got back.

We were barely down the driveway when Charity looked at me from under her curly eyelashes and said, "The real reason I came over was because I was wondering if you'd go to the Fall Ball with me."

I kinda lost control of my limbs at that point, and it was a struggle not to fall flat on my face. "You want to go with *me*?"

She smiled and bumped me with her shoulder. "Of course, silly. That's what I just said. I was hoping you'd ask me, but the dance is tomorrow night, so I decided to put it out there before somebody else did."

Before somebody else did. Haha! I hadn't felt this light-headed since the day at the fair when I rode the Eggroll six times in a row. I inhaled a long breath through my nose and blurted, "Yeah! That sounds fun." And then, for some reason, I thought of Lucy. Why did she seem so unhappy when we talked about the dance, when it could be this simple?

"Great!" Charity said. We stood there grinning and blushing at each other until she looked up at the house. "Is your mom watching us?" she whispered.

I glanced at the kitchen window, and Mom waved. Geez. "Let's go somewhere else," I suggested.

We strolled down my street, the crisp breeze cooling

my burning cheeks. Charity was gushing over the beautiful trees on our block and how they helped her not to miss the Florida weather so much. All I could think of to say in response was "Yeah" and "Uh-huh" over and over again.

"So what are you planning on wearing to the dance?"

"Uh . . . I don't know. It's my first one."

"I thought maybe we could wear something that matched. Wouldn't that be fun?"

That gave me a brilliant idea. "We *could* match! We could go as Oora and Saki! Duddy, Ike, and Wendell are taking girls, too. Let's all dress up! It's almost Halloween, so it wouldn't seem weird. I could spruce up Duddy's costume and make your Shrooms blow green smoke like mine! Wouldn't that be awesome?"

I turned to see what she thought. She'd stopped walking and was looking at me with her eyebrows raised and her mouth half open like she wanted to tell me something but it wouldn't come out.

"Oh, that won't work," I said. "I forgot you're more Team Reptile than Amphibian . . . but maybe just this once you could be Saki, since I don't think there'd be time to make you a costume by tomorrow night."

Charity put her hand on my arm and raised her eyes to mine slowly. "Todd, I was hoping we could dress up—"

"I know!" Isn't that what I'd just said?

She shook her head and smiled sweetly. "Not in costumes. I already bought a nice dress, you know. It's fuchsia, and I thought maybe we could find you a soft pink shirt and a fuchsia tie . . ."

My neck felt tight already. I pulled on my sweatshirt collar. "Fuchsia? Is that some kind of material?"

Charity smiled "You're so funny, Todd. Y'know—it's pink. I picked it because I thought it would complement your beautiful eyes and dark hair." Charity took a step closer and put her other hand on my other arm. "Wouldn't that be *special*?"

"Uh . . ." I licked my lips, which suddenly felt drier than a desert in a sandstorm. I looked around. There wasn't another soul on the street.

Charity was still watching me intently with her pool-blue eyes. But this wasn't *Dragon Sensei* anymore. I wasn't totally sure what this was.

And I needed to get back home to the Toddlians.

I swallowed and shook my head. "Uh, Charity? Maybe we could save the whole fuchsia thing for some other dance. I really have to go . . ."

"Go?"

"Uh-huh. To the bathroom!" I pulled away from her and rocketed down the block. *Is this what had made Duddy look like he had to pee in Lucy's driveway? Was this what girls did to you?*

"Tooooodd!" Charity called after me, but I didn't look back. Once I was safe inside my house, I leaned against the front door, panting. It took a minute for my stomach to settle back to normal and my breathing to slow down enough to answer Mom, who asked from the kitchen, "Todd, what was that about?"

"Just . . . homework," I mumbled, stumbling to my room. I flopped face first onto the bed and shut my eyes, trying to shut out everything about this crazy day. But it was all there, playing like a horror flick in my head: Coach Tomlin screaming, "You're not living up to your full potential!" and blasting me with icy hose water; Max kicking me in the mouth and ripping my room apart; Charity watching me with wide, serious eyes.

Everybody wanted more from me than I could give. Charity, Coach Tomlin, Lucy . . . the only one who didn't want anything from me was Duddy. Man, I missed our carefree days of goofing off and playing *Dragon Sensei*. Why was everything changing, when all I wanted was for it all to go back to the way it used to be?

To make matters worse, I couldn't even talk to Duddy about any of this mess because I hardly saw the dude anymore, now that I was on swim team and he was all gaga for Lucy.

Suddenly, an idea occurred to me. *The swim team.*

I might not be able to do anything about Duddy and Lucy, but the swim team was a different story. I'd march into Tomlin's office and quit tomorrow, like I should have done today.

I needed to slam the book shut on this weird chapter

of my life. Maybe if I hung with Duddy more I could get him to start acting like his old, non-Lucified self.

I walked to my room and slumped down on my bed feeling satisfied with my decision—quitting the team was definitely the right thing to do. But I just couldn't shake the nagging feeling that there was something I was forgetting . . .

CHAPTER 17

HERMAN

"Will Great Todd ever come back for us?" little Millicent asked into the darkness, her voice echoing against the shoebox walls.

"Of course he will, Milly," Lewis said, with more assurance than even *he* must have felt.

"What if he doesn't?" wondered Gerald the Elder. "What if we never see the light of day again?"

At that, the young Toddlians wailed with fear.

"Now hush," Persephone said gently. "Ya think I'm gonna let anythin' harm yer tiny carcasses?" She leaned over and whispered in my ear, "Herman, what's the plan?"

Lewis heard her. "I think we should stay right here

and wait on Todd to come for us. Here at least there is safety."

"And starvation!" Persephone countered.

"We may have temporarily slipped the Great One's mind," Lewis admitted. "But he will not forget us for long, I know it."

"Well, I don't!" I said passionately. "Lewis, I am sorry, but it has become quite obvious to the rest of us that we have been forsaken—"

Lewis gasped. "Please! Temporarily forgotten, maybe, but forsaken? Never!"

I stood my ground. "There can be no question about it, my friend. The time has come to take our fates into our own hands. We must load up our supplies and the creeping beasts and flying creatures."

Clarence, a new paternal person, spoke up. "Surely you are too wise, Herman, to expect me to entrust the lives of my tiny twins to a vessel that is not seaworthy."

I calmed his fears. "That is why I have completely remodeled *The Exodus,* replacing the weaker materials with sturdy corrugated cardboard from boxes in the garage. I have made extensive repairs to the hull after many middle-of-the-night visits to howtobuildaboat. com. I now know my mistake was the use of matchsticks, which were hard to keep watertight. Cardboard is all one piece, and is, after all, made of 'board,' hence the name."

Lewis objected once again. "I have seen The Adorable

One shred a material called 'cardboard' with her bare hands. Perhaps we are being hasty. Perhaps we ought to look for a sturdier materi—"

"It ain't no secret thet The Adorable One has the strength of a cyclone," Persephone interrupted. "Why, I've seen her bend a spoon into a knot with nothin' but those four teeth of hers!" She continued in a gentler tone: "Lew, you cain't deny thet yer talk with Todd was a complete bust. We're jest plumb outta options. It's sail or starve!"

Several others murmured in agreement. I heard Lewis sniffle, and my heart felt heavy. Perhaps I had been too stern. But I had been *right*.

Persephone echoed my thoughts to our friend. "Chin up, Lew! I know this is partic'lar rough on you, bein' so tenderhearted and loyal as a coon dog. But I feel mighty sure that things will look brighter soon."

Suddenly, light flooded the dark box as the lid was lifted away. We all looked up in expectation: *Had Todd come for us?*

"Well, this figures," said a high voice in our native tongue. The Adorable One peered down upon us, shaking her blond curls and muttering about the "absolute incompetence" of her elder brother.

Lewis was ecstatic at her appearance. His tears of sorrow transformed to tears of relief. He whispered to me, "I know we have agreed that Daisy is too unstable to be our god, but might we not consult her about the best way to proceed?"

Persephone nodded. "She does know a sight more about bein' human than any of us. Couldn't hurt none, and we'll need somebody to help us get the ark outta the house."

I had not considered that. "Perhaps you are right." Cupping my hands around my mouth, I yelled, "Your Adorableness, may we have a word with you?"

"Humph!" was her eloquent reply. She carried us out of the closet and set us among the building materials and effigies of infants that were strewn on her floor. Lewis had told us horrific tales of the belching effigy named Becky, and we huddled close together in the corner of the box for safety.

"O Adorable One," Lewis began, bowing. "We ask for your help today in understanding the reasoning of the human mind, which is sadly far beyond our comprehension."

Daisy stuck her pacification device in her mouth and sucked thoughtfully upon it. She nodded, and Lewis continued. "Many of my fellow Toddlians have lost faith in your brother's leadership. In fact, even I cannot help feeling he is angry with us for some reason."

Daisy spit her out pacification device long enough to ask, "Why?" then replaced it. "Nom nom nom nom."

Lewis looked down, and I placed a hand of

encouragement on his shoulder. His voice was choked with emotion as he explained our plight. "It began with his forgetting to leave us sweaty gym clothes—our main source of nourishment."

The Adorable One wrinkled her upturned nose and nodded for Lewis to carry on.

"Then Lake Parkay—our only source for water—dried up, and we nearly perished from thirst."

She scowled.

"A rotten apple, which we thought contained a message of his displeasure, was left near our peaceful hamlet, until it spawned hideous slimy creatures and enormous flying monsters who destroyed our buildings and homes, causing much distress. But all of this Lewis could have endured, had it not been for feeling that Todd no longer cared for us—no longer wanted to be *friends*."

Daisy spat out her pacification device and crossed her pudgy arms. "I am sorry to hear of your sufferings," she said kindly. "But I can't say I'm surprised. Surely you didn't think that lackadaisical lazybones was actually going to *take care* of you? Have you never heard the sad history of that unlucky crustacean, Leonardo da Pinchy?"

We told her we hadn't.

"Never mind, then. It puts me in a state of melancholy, and I'm currently completing my latest masterpiece, *Send in the Clowns*, a mixed-media piece that requires every bit of sanguine sentiment I can muster." Daisy toddled to her workstation and returned with a painting of colorful, cavorting clowns whose faces were surprisingly realistic and familiar. "I cut these faces from our last family portrait. I'm sure Mommy won't mind. Hee hee hee hee hee!"

She gave us a closer view as she laughed, and I saw she'd even made a little clown canine, using a photo of Princess VanderPuff's head.

We applauded politely, and Her Adorableness returned to the matter of our distress. "As I was saying, Todd is and ever will be a useless bumbler. The only remotely practical skill he has is break-dancing. And even there he is unfaithful. He never finished teaching me the Worm!"

"We want the Worm! We want the Worm!" chanted some of our youth, but I quieted them with a hiss: "Remember what happened the last time you asked for the Worm!"

When they were silent, Daisy concluded. "Basically, ANYONE would make a better god than my brother. Except me, of course. Although I am highly qualified, I am far too overcommitted. Why, between my artistic endeavors, playdates, meeting my never-ending nutritional needs, rearranging furniture, and keeping the parents on their toes, I scarcely have time to take a nap!"

Lewis sighed, and his shoulders slumped. He turned back to us with a downcast face, obviously disappointed that Daisy agreed with those of us who felt Todd had failed as a god. But it had been his idea to consult her in the first place, so he held his peace.

"Well, no sense sittin' around here mopin' like a bunch of lovesick longhorns. I say it's high time we put this matter to a vote. Herman?"

I nodded.

"All righty then, all in favor of ditchin' Todd and hoppin' aboard the newly spruced-up ark to find us a different god, say 'aye.'"

"AAAAYE!" shouted most of the Toddlians. Lewis hung his head and choked out a "nay."

Clearly, the "ayes" carried the vote, and as much as it hurt me to see my friend Lewis pained, I had to think of the greater good, which was to find a greater god.

While we voted, The Adorable One had been studying a cylindrical device she had pulled from her box of toys. The inside contained a blue liquid, and the outside was marked with lines and numbers.

She interrupted our departure plans. "Please, my little friends, let me assist you in your voyage!" The crazed look she had worn when she had "helped" us test sail *The Exodus* was upon her face once more. "According to My First Barometer here, it's supposed to rain tomorrow. Which means the rushing river that runs beside our front yard should be flowing along splendidly. Pleeeaaase?"

With that entreaty, Daisy peered into the shoebox with enormous brown eyes that didn't look altogether sane. I was reminded of a Shakespeare quote: "O, mischief, thou art swift to enter in the thoughts of desperate men."

The Adorable One was explaining her plans to sneak us out of the house tomorrow when the maternal person was occupied with a piano lesson. She would then deposit us in the River Drain by the curb, and we could sail away to make a new beginning.

It was getting late, and Daisy hospitably offered to let us spend the evening on her Blankie. We all felt what an honor she had conferred upon us and accepted happily. Of course, she also had to sleep with the Blankie, so we nestled down on its luxurious filth inside the bars of her white cage.

Daisy-related dirt was the next best thing to Todd dirt, and we gorged ourselves on sweet, sticky grunge until our entrails nearly exploded. We were too full to talk much, and I settled into the comfort of the Blankie's worn, unwashed fibers full of hope and anticipation for the next day's journey.

I awakened from my dozing to hear someone whimpering nearby. *Lewis?* I rose to comfort him, but Persephone intercepted me. "Best leave him by his lonesome and let him have his cry out. He'll come 'round to the idea in his own time."

She was right, of course, but my bed was not nearly so soft when I settled back into it.

CHAPTER 18

The next morning was Friday, the day of the dance. Before homeroom, I paced back and forth outside Coach Tomlin's office, practicing my quitting speech before I went in. I really wished I'd taken two minutes and scarfed down some cereal or something before I'd left home. My stomach was churning, and I felt shaky.

How should I say it? Should I just flat out beg for mercy? I called up my newly acquired acting skills—wringing my hands and putting on a pitiful face with puppy-dog eyes. Hey, sometimes it worked on Mom . . . "Pleeeease, Coach Tomlin, sir, let me off the team," I whispered. "As you saw yesterday, I'm an unworthy athlete, and I will only bring shame and humiliation to the

WAVES." Here I hung my head and slumped my shoulders. "Some of us just aren't born to swim."

Naw, that would never work. He'd probably tell me to quit being a wuss, do thirty crunches, and drink another protein shake. But it's not like I could tell him the truth: that I wanted more time to spend with my civilization of little bug-like people who worshipped me as a god, and to discuss boogers and *Dragon Sensei* with my best friend.

Gulp. At the thought of the Toddlians, my stomach clenched so hard I was actually kinda lucky that I hadn't eaten breakfast. *I left them in Daisy's closet!* I groaned—Daisy had sure as heck woken up from her nap by now, and there was a good chance she'd find the strange shoebox in her closet. She seemed as weirdly organized as I was messy. Clearly we'd inherited different genes.

And what would Daisy do with the Toddlians? Oh, man, I didn't even want to think about it. *If the way she treats my* Dragon Sensei *figurines is any sign . . .*

I had to get home ASAP. Which meant I *really* needed off the WAVES—and fast. Maybe I could come up with a sob story. I mean, my life wasn't perfect. Surely there were some good, heartstrings-pulling reasons I shouldn't be on the team.

"Coach Tomlin, I'd love to stay on the swim team, but my schedule is too full. Middle school is hard, and I need to spend more time on my studies. If my grades slip, you'd only have to kick me off the team anyway. Besides, my dad is working overtime at the hospital, and my mom is so stressed since she was laid off from teaching that *she* may end up in the hospital with a nervous breakdown, and she really needs me to help babysit my little sister . . ." No, that was slipping into pitiful mode again, and Coach Tomlin didn't seem to be especially inclined toward sympathy.

The best approach was probably to be tough, like the coach himself. That seemed to be the language he understood. I scowled and frowned, quietly yelling, "You can keep your dumb chuck-ups and piggyback stair runs! You can keep your rotten hosedowns!" I pointed at the door and whisper-screamed, *"YOU CAN KEEP YOUR STUPID SWIM TEAM, TOMLIN! I QUIT!"*

"You wanna say that to my face, Buttrock?"

I must've jumped a foot in the air. How I didn't pee myself, I'll never know. I whirled around to face The Ogre, who apparently was not in his office like I'd thought. For a moment, I wished I were teeny-tiny, like a Toddlian. It would make hiding in a situation like this a heckuva lot easier.

Coach Tomlin's steely eyes bored into mine as his face turned to granite. "You wanna quit my team, boy? Is that what you said?"

I backpedaled into the door, stammering, "I . . . well, that is . . . I . . ."

"Inside," he ordered, pushing me out of the way and unlocking the door. I followed him into his lit office. Except for some motivational posters on the walls, the room was almost bare. There was, however, a metal chair across from his desk. I started to sit in it when Coach bellowed, "Who said you could sit down? Stand up and answer me like a man!"

I stood rigidly and focused my eyes on a poster behind his desk. It was of a grimacing bodybuilder struggling to lift a ginormous barbell. The caption said PAIN IS YOUR FRIEND.

Coach Tomlin walked around behind his desk and crossed his arms. "Now tell me again how you're gonna quit my team." His low, controlled voice was scarier than any of his shouting.

There was no other option; I had to give him my speech. And like the lily-liver I was, I went the sappy route. "Pleeeeease, Coach. I need off the team. I'm needed at home. My dad has to work nights, and my mom is a stress muffin trying to make ends meet and deal with my diabolical baby sister." I glanced up at him then, which was a mistake, and went on, "And you said yourself, sir, that I'm not a good swimmer—"

"I never said that! Look at me, boy." I met his stony gaze. "I never said you weren't a good swimmer. I said you weren't living up to your potential. And it's my job to get you to do so. You hear me?"

I nodded.

Coach Tomlin came around to the front of the desk and leaned his butt on it. "If you quit now, you'll never know how good of a swimmer you could have become. It's my *duty* to keep you on this team and help you realize your inner strength, Buttrock. Thank me."

I knew it was a bad idea, but I had to keep arguing. "I just—"

"BUTTROCK!"

The nickname was like a clap of thunder shaking the whole office and literally bringing me to my knees. "Yes, sir?" I whispered.

Coach Tomlin leaned down and got in my face, not even seeming surprised that he'd just knocked me off my feet using *only his voice.* "Do you know what responsibility is?"

I gulped. *Apparently not?* "Ah, I think so, sir."

He leaned in closer, so I could smell his breath. He wasn't a coffee drinker, it seemed. He kind of smelled like Gatorade. "You have a gift, Buttrock. A real, God-given gift for swimming. Don't you think—since you're lucky enough to have this talent—that it's your *responsibility* to develop it? What if you're on a sinking cruise ship and you're the only hope of getting people safely to the lifeboats? What if your best friend—that milquetoast I've seen you with in the hallways, the one with his finger in his nose—what if he were to fall into a

swift-moving current and drown, *Buttrock*? You'd want
to save him, wouldn't you? *Wouldn't* you?"

I flashed back to the WAVES tryouts. I *had* saved
Duddy then, but that was just in four feet of still water—
not a swift-moving current. Maybe Coach Tomlin had a
point.

I'd done a pitiful job of living up to my responsibili-
ties to the Toddlians lately. But maybe it wasn't only the
Toddlians who needed me.

Maybe I had a responsibility to myself, too. "Okay,
sir," I whispered.

"What's that?" Coach Tomlin barked.

"OKAY, SIR!" I yelled, straightening up. Then I
remembered. "THANK YOU, SIR!"

For the first time ever, I saw a hint of a smile on the
man's face. "Good. I'll make a man of you yet. Show up
at the meet this afternoon ready to swim your guts out,
or you'll see why they call me *Terrifying* Coach Tomlin."

Dark storm clouds were gathering as the final bell
rang, matching my mood. I'd decided to stay on the
swim team, but as the day wore on, I was getting more
and more worried about the Toddlians. Even if Daisy
hadn't gotten to them, they had to be freaked out,
stuck in that dark shoebox for this long with no food or
water . . . It made me feel terrible. After Coach Tomlin's

speech that morning, I believed I did have a responsibility to the team. But honoring that responsibility meant letting down the Toddlians, again. My life was getting way too complicated, and all I wanted was to make it simple again.

With that in mind, I'd decided not to talk to *anybody* while I was at the pool, especially not Charity, who I'd artfully avoided all day. (Okay, maybe not "artfully." In art class she'd come up to ask what time to pick me up tonight, and I'd swallowed an entire bottle of red tempera paint, getting myself sent to the nurse's office. But I just *really* didn't want to think about the dance, for some reason.)

I got dressed in one of the locker room stalls, which took awhile because there were about a jillion kids from different schools crammed in with us. When I came out into the pool room, I saw our team crowded around Coach Tomlin's office door. I joined them right as he came out of the office and blew his whistle.

"Okay, WAVES, I've got a special announcement, so listen up." At that moment there was a rumble of thunder so loud, we all jumped a little. Except Tomlin himself, who scowled at the ceiling like he was personally offended. "As I was saying, I've decided to reinstate Mr. Loving as a team member, and I expect you to welcome him accordingly. Thank me."

WHAAAAAAT?!

I did *not* thank him along with everyone else. I don't

even think I remembered to breathe. It was one of those horrifying moments when the room spins and everything around you sounds real far away. The only thing I could think of was that if I died, Max would get the Toddlians for sure. And I couldn't let that happen.

I shook my head and managed a breath. Everyone was staring toward the bleachers, and I turned to see Max swagger down to us like he was some kind of hero. He strutted over and stood next to the coach, aping his crossed arms.

Was Coach Tomlin insane? What about Max trying to incinerate us all?

"Mr. Loving stopped by my office today and cleared up the little matter of a certain pool fire," the coach said. "I'm now convinced it was merely an accident, blown out of proportion by Madame Dauphinee's delicate composition. We'll say no more about it. Am I understood?"

"YES, SIR!" the others yelled. I was too steamed to even mouth the words.

While I was stretching my arms behind my head, Max came up and almost yanked one out of the socket. "It's so nice to see ya, loser," he whispered, snapping the elastic strap on my goggles. He still had my right arm pinned behind my back, and I stomped on his foot with everything I had.

"Ow!" he yelped as he let go. "You're gonna pay for that, dork!"

Charity broke away from the girls and confronted Max. "Leave him alone, Loving!"

Max snorted. "Oh, how sweet. Here she comes to defend her wimpy-butt boyfriend."

Charity ignored him and touched my sore arm. "You okay, Todd? Are we still on for tonight?"

Gulp.

Max's unibrow lowered menacingly, and he barged in between Charity and me. "Better swim fast, Little Butty." He poked my chest. "Better swim for your life."

I planned on it. Max had made my world a living nightmare since Day One of middle school, and I was going to make him eat my wake just like he had at try-outs. After all, what did I have to lose? If he ended up killing me, at least I'd go out with a bang.

I slunk away from Charity, ignoring her confused stare. Max and I ended up in lanes next to each other for the boys' freestyle, and for once I was glad. As I stood on the blocks, all the swirling frustration, fear, anger, and humiliation I'd been feeling gelled into pure adrenaline. I bent over, gripped the edge of the platform, and shut my eyes. For one moment I let myself feel the crushing grip of Max's fist around my throat. That was all the fuel I needed.

When the gun went off for the fifty-meter freestyle, I sprang like a cheetah into my dive. I didn't look any-where but ahead when I surfaced, and I only breathed twice the first lap; I was a machine focused on one goal.

Stroke, stroke, stroke . . . I sliced through the pool until I got to the wall. A super-tight kick turn, and I shot like a missile under the water. This time when I breathed I glanced at the lane on my right. Max still hadn't reached the turn.

I went into warp speed, summoning every ounce of strength I possessed, kicking like a maniac, until I reached out and touched the wall.

I popped up and saw that Max was still way down his lane. My muscles burned and I was exhausted, but the exhilaration of beating Max publicly was sweet indeed. When I looked around, I saw I hadn't just beaten him, I'd beaten *everybody*!

That's when I heard the cheers. The WAVES were going wild, and when I saw the clock, I understood why. 26:51! *Whoa.*

Charity ran up as soon as I was out of the water and gave me a hug. Somehow I didn't mind it. I even hugged her back.

Coach Tomlin was clearly impressed. He draped a towel around my shoulders and asked, "You think you can hustle like that three more times?"

"Yessir," I panted. And I did. Powered by a strange feeling I'd never felt before—call it a winning mentality or whatever you want—I won the one-hundred meter *and* the two-hundred meter! *And* I helped the WAVES nail the relay. It was turning out to be a day of miracles.

At the end of the meet Coach Tomlin put the

first-place medal around my neck and actually *smiled* at me. The crowd chanted, "BU-TROCHE! BU-TROCHE!" for what felt like five minutes. My cheeks hurt from grinning so hard; I'd never experienced anything quite like it.

After a lot of handshaking and attaboys from other swimmers and coaches, I rushed to the locker room to change. But Charity spotted me and left the group she was with to come over to me. For a minute she just smiled and shook her head in silence. Finally she said, "Todd Butroche, you are absolutely amazing. To swim like that after what Max did to your arm . . ." My shoulder was hurting pretty bad by that point, but I was too stoked to give it much thought. "I was a little weirded out when you didn't talk to me all day. But now I realize you were just psyching yourself up to compete. Tonight, I am going to be so proud to walk into that dance with the best swimmer in the district."

The dance. That was one problem my victory here wasn't going to solve. But how bad could it be? I liked Charity, right? "Um, I gotta go."

"Sure." She grabbed my hand and gave it a quick squeeze. "But be sure to wear your medal later." With that she was off to go "get ready."

Once I was changed, a few more kids stopped me to check out my medal, which was super sweet, with a guy swimming inside a gold ring. But I was already making my way out the door. There was no time to waste; my other big responsibility needed me!

Before I could get out, though, Coach Tomlin pulled me aside. "You made me proud out there today, son. This morning you wanted to throw in the towel, but you dug down deep and found your inner strength. Not only did you not quit, but you performed like a champ."

I was itching to get changed and get out of there, but Coach Tomlin's words were like a sticky honey, molding me to the spot. Was I dreaming?

His normally stony face melted into a grin. "I knew I was right to put you through the wringer, Butroche. Some kids would have cracked under the pressure, but not you. You always had the potential to go the distance. And now I think you've got the heart to take you there as well." He thumped me on the back, sending my sore shoulder into a spasm of pain.

I winced and said, "Thank you, sir!" I could not believe how good that made me feel. I felt something that I hadn't felt lately, especially in the last couple of days: proud to be Todd Butroche.

But I'd be even prouder once I rescued the Toddlians.

CHAPTER 19

Of course Max had to show up and try to ruin my moment before I could even make it to my locker. He grabbed my medal and pulled the ribbon taut, chafing my neck. "Gonna take this home to show your little buggy friends?"

I reached out to take the medal, but he grabbed me by the wrist. "Oh, yes, I know you sent me home with an empty sock . . . *again.* But it's only a matter of time, Buttrock. You can't hide them forever."

Max's threats just reinforced that I needed to get home as fast as I could. I ignored him and grabbed my clothes.

"And then the little bug-people will be mine!" Max was saying. Then, right there in front everybody, he leaned his head back and cackled, "MUA HA HA HA!"

Seriously?

I yanked my medal away from him and shoved him mid-laugh. He taunted me while I threw on my clothes, saying he was going to pour salt on my "little friends" and see if they melted like slugs; cover them alive in molten chocolate and sell them as candied ants; tie them individually to firecrackers . . .

I ignored him and scurried outside. A huge storm must have come through—there were leaves, branches, and trash strewn all over the streets. It was still raining a little, though it looked like the worst had passed. Max trailed me all the way home, making threats. "You think you're hot stuff now that you've won a medal? Big deal. The only reason you swim fast is because you're so tiny—just like your little buggy buddies that I'm going to run over with my brother's Camero . . ."

One advantage of being tiny is that you can outrun overgrown man-children. I ran my buns off, and while at first I just barely managed to stay a few yards ahead of Max, by the time we got to my street I had a lead of a few houses. He ranted all the way to my house, but I couldn't understand what he was saying. By then, he was red and panting. When I reached my front door, the rain had stopped. I turned and watched Max stagger up to the driveway, gasping for air. He shook his fist at me, and I answered with a shrug before I went inside.

I sprinted into Daisy's room and nearly tripped over

something on her cluttered floor. I started to kick it out of the way when I realized what it was. The shoebox!

My heart sank. It was empty.

"Hey, guys, are you in here somewhere?" I listened for a minute, but when I didn't hear anything I went after Daisy. "Daisy! Where are you?" I called, looking in the bathroom and my room. Mom was in the kitchen putting biscuits in the oven. "Have you seen Daisy?" I asked her.

"What's she done now?" was Mom's weary response. "I just finished changing her wet clothes and put *Brainy Baby* on for her in the living room. Hey! What's that medal about?"

I didn't take time to answer. She didn't know there'd been a swim meet because I hadn't bothered to tell her, since I hadn't planned on being at it.

Daisy was in the living room, making some kind of sculpture out of remotes and old VHS tapes while *Brainy Baby* sang about molecular structures in the background. Her creation looked surprisingly like a ship. *Weird.*

I decided not to yell at her, since that never did any good. Kneeling down beside her, I asked, "Daisy, have you seen the Toddlians? They're a bunch of people about this big." She wouldn't look at me, just kept repositioning remotes and sucking on her Binky with that infuriating "nom nom nom."

I resorted to bribery. "Look, Daisy," I coaxed, taking

off the medal and dangling it in front of her. "You can wear Toddy's necklace if you'll show me where you put the little people."

She grabbed the medal with her free hand, studied it for half a second, and then hurled it across the living room. This was going nowhere. I picked up the medal and ran back to the kitchen. "Mom, did you see Daisy playing with a shoebox today?"

Mom stopped punching numbers on the microwave and stared at the ceiling. "Noooo, but she did somehow get out in the rain and was playing with a little paper boat by the end of the driveway while I was doing dishes a while ago. I must've left the door unlocked when I went out to get the mail. Almost gave me a heart attack. She could've . . ."

A little paper boat. Could it be the Toddlians? Had they somehow gotten onto Daisy's toy and been taken for a sail in the gutter?

I didn't have time to think it all out. I barreled out the door and down the driveway, ignoring Max, who was kicked back on our porch swing. I heard the swing hit the brick as he jumped off, but my eyes were focused on the swirling, raging gutters.

Sure enough, there was a miniature cardboard boat in the gutter near the drive. It was tiny—too tiny to be Daisy's toy—and it was floating away from me. My heart raced as I ran toward it. *The Toddlians made this.*

If they'd wanted to take a boat ride, why hadn't they just asked for my help? *Why would they leave without telling me?* I ran after the boat. No way was that cardboard going to keep its shape once it got really wet. *Oh, no . . .*

Lewis's heartbroken face from the day before flashed through my mind, and it hit me. They *had* tried to tell me. But I hadn't been listening, and the sick feeling in my gut told me I'd missed something major.

Max was breathing down my neck by this time, blathering on, blowtorch, dismembering, blah blah blah, but I didn't really comprehend what he was saying. I chased after the Toddlians as they sped toward the drain, Max on my heels.

It looked like the cardboard boat was already beginning to absorb water and buckle. And now the drain was only a few yards away; the Toddlians had finally seen it. They were screaming their tiny lungs out. "GREEEAAAT TOOODD!"

I wouldn't fail them this time!

"Wait a minute, Buttrock," Max wheezed behind me, "they're on that boat, aren't they? That's why you want it so badly . . ."

I didn't answer, lunging for the boat right before it reached the drain and had it in my grasp. The Toddlians cheered. "I got you!" I shouted.

Max's combat boot pressed onto my forearm, pinning

me to the ground. My hand opened under the pressure, and the Toddlians floated out.

"No you don't," he said. Max sat on my back, then leaned over and flicked the boat toward the drain. "Bon voyage, buggy people!" he cried with sick glee.

I watched in horror as the boat was sucked into a vortex of whirling water right in front of the drain. The Toddlians screamed, and I fought with everything in me to push Max off my back, but I couldn't budge him. In the end I watched helplessly as my people were shot out of the whirlpool and disappeared down the drain, crying, "GREEEAAAT TOOOOODD!"

CHAPTER 20
PERSEPHONE

"AAAUUUGGGHHH!" we hollered as we tumbled through the air, water sloshin' us from every direction. How none of us fell out is more than I can figger; we grabbed onto the sides of our ship as best we could, but they done got mighty soggy 'n' slippery. Still, when we finally hit the bottom of that big black hole, somehow we'd all managed to make it. *Kersploosh!* went the ark into a ginormous river, and the current pulled us along helter-skelter through the darkness. We'd landed in a chamber that was black as a midnight with no moon. I could tell it was a chamber on account of the way our screams bounced around.

Speakin' of bouncin' around, that's jest what we'd

been doin' since we made the terrible mistake of letting Daisy plop us in that little river outside her house. I hadn't been out of Todd's yard since the time I wrangled a squirrel. I'd plumb forgot how wild and wooly the big world was. We were no match for it.

And *The Exodus 2.0*, refurbished though it was, weren't no match whatsoever for the powerful current that drew us downriver like a cowboy reelin' in a tied calf. Herman realized that as soon as he tried to steer us down the little river. His cardboard rudder had snapped off in his hand, and he'd ordered us to "abandon ship!"

Well, that would've been suicide, and I convinced everybody to hang tight to whatever they could cling to. What we *shoulda* hung tight to was our faith in Todd. He actually appeared, jest like Lewis had said he would, and tried to save our sorry carcasses! Lew had been right all along, but the rest of us were in such a goldurn hurry to make somethin' happen . . . and look where it had landed us.

"Where *are* we?" little Milly whimpered as we whirled like a rank bull through the dark, echoing place.

"I ain't sure," I said, patting her wet head, "but don't you worry none. Persephone's right here."

The boat suddenly quit spinnin', and I raised my voice above the caterwaulin'. "I know it's a sight too late to be sayin' this, but we were wrong to doubt Todd. I'm sure sorry I ever . . ."

"No time for apologies now," Herman panted. "We must find out how to appease His Greatness and make this swirling stop." He went all white and declared, "Since this entire scheme was my idea, I volunteer to sacrifice myself, as a figurative Jonah, to the angry waves."

None of us had any idea what he was yammerin' about, but when he made like he was gonna fling himself over the side of the boat, I lassoed him, then lashed him to the ark's steerin' wheel, which hadn't been any more use than the rudder. "What kinda fool stunt was that?" I hissed. "Yer the only one of us thet knows anything about this blamed boat, and you ain't sacrificin' *nothin'*!"

Just then the current started its crazy do-si-do again, and I looked at Herman. *Thet was it!* "Nobody move!" I yelled to the people who were crashin' into each other and rollin' all over the place. One by one I lashed them to each other and the deck, thankful I'd at least had the sense to bring a whole spool of floss.

Once everyone was anchored to the deck, I tied Lewis and myself to the broken rudder. He was bellyachin' and boohooin' about how he should've tried harder to convince us thet this whole exodus was wrong. "We should have trusted him," he wailed. "Great Todd would never have let such a thing happen to us."

Thet set everybody else bawlin' again and sayin', "We're sorry, O Great One! Please save us!" and such.

"STOP IT!" I ordered. "We ain't got time for thet now! All our strength needs to be focused on gettin' outta this place alive!"

"But where *are* we?" Milly cried again.

Herman's shuddery voice rose above the crash of the waves and the yowling and flapping of the skeered bugs beneath us. "My friends, I fear we have entered the Underworld of the Greek myths Lucy told us about. I fear we are riding Charon's boat upon the River Styx . . . en route to Hades itself!"

CHAPTER 21

I shoved Max off me with some kind of supernatural strength. He fell onto his back and into the street. I straddled his chest and grabbed him by his meaty neck. "You big dumb ape—that's all you are!—I'm going to make you regret pushing my friends down that drain!" I growled. My own strength scared me, and from the way his unibrow shot into his hair and his beady eyes bugged out, it scared him, too. "I'll get you for this," I seethed as I loosened my grip, "later."

I hopped off him and rocketed back down the block to the only person who might be able to help me. Every second wasted brought the Toddlians closer to doom.

I had to bang on Lucy's door for a minute before she answered. Had she seen me coming? Was she avoiding me after our weird late-night conversation about the dance? I was about to run around to her bedroom window when she opened the door.

"Oh, hey, Todd!" she said, looking surprised. Her hair was all done up in curls. She tilted her head toward the house. "I was just picking out my shoes for the dance tonight. My mom said I could borrow a pair of her heels, but I have no idea what public school kids wear! Maybe you can help me—"

"I need you!" I blurted. She didn't know where to look after that. "I mean, I need you to help me save our civilization. Max pushed the Toddlians down the sewer drain, and you have to help me get down there and save them!"

Lucy's pink cheeks paled. She gulped and hissed, "They're in the sewer? Todd, how could you let things go this far?"

It felt like she'd slapped me, but I knew I deserved it.

"Todd, *when* will you learn to be responsible and care for them properly?" she asked. "I had thought—"

"I know, I know! But we don't have time for this now. How can we get into the sewer?"

Lucy shook her head. "Impossible! Those drains are all locked down tight." She chewed her cheek for a minute, then said, "Our only hope is to figure out where that water reenters the system . . ."

"I don't get it."

"It doesn't matter." Her eyes lit up, and the color

came back into her cheeks. "C'mon!" she said, running down the hall to her room. "Do you have a rubber ducky?"

A *rubber ducky*? "Uh, sure, Daisy has one."

"Perfect!" Lucy rummaged around on her desk and grabbed something, put it in her jeans pocket, then snatched her iPad off her bed and shoved it in her backpack. "Let's roll!"

We beat it across the street to my house and snagged the ducky. Lucy started fiddling with it right there in the bathroom. We hurried to the drain, and she turned the ducky over, implanting a tiny device into the hole in its base.

"What is that?"

Lucy talked as she manipulated the device to make sure it was snug. "This is a GPS I was using to test my cesium clock. Once we drop ducky here into the storm drain, we can track where the water—and the Toddlian boat—is going."

Wow, I always knew she was smart, but . . . wow. "Lucy, you are a genius!"

She smiled a little but didn't look up. "Thanks. But I actually stole this idea off an episode of *Veronica Mars*. That girl is legit."

I had no idea who she was talking about and didn't waste time by asking. She pulled her iPad out of her backpack and started typing. "We're right here," she said, pointing at the aerial-view map on the screen. "And this little blue dot moving east is the ducky. It's already under Helen Avenue, and they had quite a head start . . ."

"Let's go!" I said, yanking on her arm.

"Hold on, we have to see where the water comes out. Mm-hmm, mm-hmm. Okay, the sewer empties into the Little Molasses River between Laurel Lane and Eighth Avenue. That's not far. But we'd better hurry; it looks like the ducky's moving at an alarming rate."

"Huh?"

"It's picking up speed." She tucked the iPad under her arm. "Follow me!"

We cut across yards for two streets, which brought us to Helen Avenue. Lucy checked the map, and we zig-zagged down north-south side streets until we reached Laurel Lane. "If we hurry we can probably make it before they emerge from the sewer. We're way ahead of the ducky. Three blocks that way."

I nodded, trying to ignore the stabbing stitch in my side.

Lucy stowed the iPad in her backpack, and I pumped my legs and arms for all they were worth. She kept up with me, her black braids flying out behind her like wings.

We were on the outskirts of our neighborhood now, running parallel to the rushing river. At the Eighth

Avenue bridge we had to stop to wait for a stream of cars to pass, because you couldn't access the river from the side we were on. "C'mon," I muttered. The cars just kept whizzing by. "Forget this." I zipped between two cars, and from the honking I heard behind me, I knew Lucy had done the same.

Beneath the bridge the storm drain spewed into the river. "There!" Lucy panted as we scrambled down the bank. Sure enough, the round drain hole was built into the bottom side of the bridge. Only there were *two* openings, one in each side.

"You watch that one," I said, pointing to the hole on the right. "And I'll watch this one."

All we could do now was wait . . . and hope we weren't too late.

CHAPTER 22
LEWIS

We whirled madly down the dark river that Herman thought was our passage to the afterlife. I clung to Persephone, who was yelling for everyone to keep their chins up, "and if you have to retch, for the love of Pete, aim down!"

Suddenly, the spinning slowed but the current sped up. We were sailing in a straight line toward . . . was that a light? Yes! We all cheered as the ark sped steadily toward a bright white spot in the distance.

Maybe Herman had been right; maybe we were making our final voyage into that great unknown. But somehow the brightness warmed my chilled bones as it drew me toward it, like a mother's sweet embrace. I knew then that if our time should come, I would not be afraid of death. Todd had brought us into the light, and I would remember my happy times with him as my own lamp went out.

These pleasant thoughts were interrupted by the most extraordinary experience! Without warning, the ark shot out into the brilliant sunlight and for the briefest moment was suspended in midair.

Gerald the Elder cried, "Is this the eeeeeend?" Then the screams of a desperate people rose to the skies.

Would Todd hear us?

We plummeted end over end down a spectacular waterfall. I gripped the floss with one hand and Persephone with the other. As fast as we flew down the surface of the glassy water, the whole scene played itself out in slow motion before me. I remember briefly catching Persephone's eyes and seeing my reflection in their inky depths. Somehow I knew in that moment we would always be bound together, whether in life . . . or death.

This surreal and beautiful realization was quenched as we plunged beneath the icy waves of the enormous river below us. This certainly was no fiery River Styx! No! All the fire was in my lungs, which burned for air. We seemed to be moving both forward and upward as we churned in circles beneath the surface. Would we clear the water in time? Or were we like the damned from Herman's stories, submerged in water under the ire of our god? Would my people and I perish as one, without a chance to tell Todd we were sorry for doubting him?

My limbs were numb and my head close to explosion when suddenly we popped back into the glorious glow! Oh, sweet oxygen!

"Is everyone all right?" Persephone shouted. All were accounted for, although drenched and quaking with cold as they lay strewn across the deck. We cheered once again through chattering teeth . . . except Herman. He was examining *The Exodus* with worried eyes.

Then I saw it, too: the ark was absorbing water and buckling dangerously. We were perilously low in the water. "Herman?" I called above the happy voices. From across the deck I saw him swallow and shake his head.

We had been spared, only to be doomed once more. *Oh, Todd! Please do not forsake us now!* My earlier state of resignation had disappeared beneath the swirling waters. I wanted to live! To marry! To hear the tiny pitter-patter of—

"What in tarnation?" Persephone cried.

I followed her gaze.

TODD! Salvation! He was running along the bank of the river, waving! He had seen us! He had been pursuing us all this time we had been despairing!

"Don't worry, guys!" he called. "I'm coming to get you!"

Tears mingled with the river water on my cheeks as my heart overflowed with happiness. *He has not forgotten us!*

CHAPTER 23

We didn't have to wait long. Lucy elbowed me in the ribs and pointed. The Toddlians' soggy boat shot out of the drain on the right and went airborne. I could have sworn I heard *GERONIMO!* mingled with tiny screams as the boat rode the waterfall to the swirling river below.

Lucy gasped as the boat disappeared for a second, then cried out as it popped back to the surface, pointing. It was moving crazy fast in the strong current. Now I *knew* I heard screaming, even over the rushing of the water.

Without thinking, I ran along the riverbank and peeled off my heavy sweater, calling to my people. Lucy followed me, yelling, "Todd! You're not thinking of going

in there? Don't do it! That current is too strong for you!"
I kicked off my shoes. "The water's too cold!"

I heard her shout something about "hypothermia"
and "concussion" as I dove in. The freezing cold water
took my breath away. Still, I propelled myself to the top
and scanned the surface of the water, which was glitter-
ing in the light of the setting sun. There! The boat was
spinning in circles about ten yards ahead of me.

I started to swim toward it, but the current caught
me and dragged me back under. My arms and legs were
going numb from the cold, and my lungs burned as
invisible forces sucked me downriver.

No matter how hard I struggled, I couldn't get enough
momentum with my sluggish arms to make it back to
the surface. My lungs were on fire, my body was frozen,
and I knew this was it. Not only was I going to lose the
Toddlians, I was going to lose my life, too—just when I'd
found something I was good at.

A sharp object slammed me in the back, knocking
the wind out of me. I sucked in a breath and looked
around, reaching out to grab hold of whatever I'd run
into. It was a tree limb! I pulled myself on top of it and
inhaled deeply.

But where were the Toddlians? I couldn't get a visual
on the boat. Had it been swept under by the current too?
I pushed off the branch and started swimming upriver.
I had to fight the current with every stroke. It seemed

almost like I was swimming in place, but I kicked my frozen feet as hard as I possibly could. My sneakers were like lead weights.

Every five or six strokes I'd stop and look around real quick. This caused me to drift back downriver, but I had to find them. I was on the verge of giving up on this approach and going back on land to try to sight them from the bank, when I saw the dilapidated boat teetering on the edge of a protruding rock.

It didn't look good. Were the Toddlians still alive? Had they been killed on impact when they hit the rock? I strained my ears, but the sounds of the swirling water drowned out everything else.

Swim, Todd! my brain told my numb body. Mechanically, I swam toward the rock. Now I could hear them screaming . . . *my name!* The boat rocked danger-ously, and I willed my legs to kick harder. *Al-most there! Al-most there!* I thought with each stroke. I made it to the rock just as the boat began to fall—reaching out of the water to catch it just in time.

The Toddlians cheered as I struggled to the bank, cra-dling their vessel.

I climbed the slippery bank and was pulled the last few feet by Lucy, holding my people gently in my hands. They were still cheering. "Are you okay?" she said, wrap-ping her red hoodie around me.

My teeth were chattering so bad I had trouble talking.

"Y-y-yeah. H-h-how about y-you guys?" I lifted the Toddlians to eye level. "Are y-you okay?"

"HAIL, GREAT TODD! HAIL, GREAT TODD!" was their reply. Lewis's voice was the loudest.

"E-everybody st-still in the b-boat?" I squinted down at them and could just barely make out who was who.

Herman climbed out onto my hand. "All present and accounted for, Your Greatness. Except for some of the winged insects, who grew faint of heart and flew to find their own fates."

Lewis scampered up my wet sleeve and stood on my shoulder. "I knew you'd come for us, Great Todd," he whispered. "Thank you!"

Something kind of choked me then, and I was glad my face was wet so Lucy wouldn't see my tears.

Persephone jumped up on my arm, too. "Let's whoop it up for rootin' tootin' Todd!" she hollered. "HAIL, GREAT TODD! HAIL, GREAT TODD!" The others, including Lucy, joined her.

We headed back to my house, laughing like we were glad to be alive, which we were. When we reached the driveway, I put my hand on Lucy's shoulder and waited until she met my eyes. "Thank you. I hope you know I never could've done any of this without you." I was starting to tear up again, but this time I didn't care. "You're such a good friend to me, Lucy. I mean that."

Lucy dropped her dark eyes and turned pink. "You're

not so bad yourself," she said to her shoes, and then she looked up at me with wide, sincere brown eyes as she murmured, "Your friendship means a lot to me, Todd. I mean . . . *you* mean a lot to me."

I was kind of speechless at that, and Lucy seemed a little uncomfortable too—she blushed and cleared her throat. "Anyway, well, I'd better go; I have to finish getting ready for the dance," she said, giving me a hesitant glance before looking down again. "With Duddy."

Right. The dance. As she walked away I heard my front door open. "Todd Butroche!" came my mother's voice. "You look soaked to the skin!"

CHAPTER 24

LEWIS

Is there anything sweeter than coming home? I thought not, especially after nearly losing my home this day, along with my god.

Herman, Persephone, and I were huddled up in a snuggly bit of cotton fluff Todd had extracted from one of Daisy's dismembered teddy bears. He had placed us on his pillow, and we were going to have what he called a "heart-to-heart" talk. I liked the sound of that.

I sipped on my Lego head of warm Todd sweat, closing my eyes in delight.

Todd lay upon his belly on the bed, so he could be eye level with us. He pulled his micro-glasses over his eyes and asked, "Now what in the world possessed you guys to build a boat and try to sail it in the gutter? You nearly drowned!"

I spoke before the others had a chance. "Great Todd live forever—"

"You don't have to keep calling me that, Lew. Just plain Todd's fine."

I nodded. "Just Plain Todd, forgive us, but we thought you were angry with our people. As I told you before, we believed that we had so displeased you that you left the sign of the Red Thing for us as a message, and when we could not decipher it, sent the fearsome flying goggle-eyed creatures to punish us."

"Red thing?" Todd furrowed his brow, and then nodded. "Oh, right, the apple."

"Some of us took it into our noggins that you were trying to tell us somethin' by letting it get all nastified," Persephone said. She was kind enough not to name names.

I sipped some more sweat and cleared my throat. "But that is not all, Great—Just Plain Todd. We were suffering from hunger . . . and thirst at your recent neglect." I lowered my eyes, pained to have to say this to one I reverenced. "You never seemed to have time for your people, and we felt . . . we felt—"

"Don't cry, Lewis," Todd said softly.

Was I crying? I suppose I was.

He went on, "I never neglected you because I was

mad. You should know by now that when I'm mad I stomp around and yell a lot. When have I ever left you some crazy complicated message?"

He had a point.

"It's just that with school, and swim team, and . . . well, anyway, I got really busy." Now he cleared *his* throat. "Too busy. And I promise you, it won't happen again. If it even looks like I'm starting to ignore you, or forget to leave you sweaty clothes or fill your water dish, I'm counting on you"—he pointed at each of us—"to come talk to me about it. And if you guys do something wrong, like have a wild party and trash my room, well, you bet I'm gonna call you on it."

I could tell he was kidding, but I had to correct him on one point.

"I *did* try talking to you."

"I know. And I'm so sorry I didn't get what you were saying. But when that happens, you have to keep trying! Like Persephone says, I have beans for brains, you know." He smiled, and it warmed me more than all the cotton-fluff comforters in the world. "But seriously, if there's one thing I know, it's that you can't give up, especially not on people." His eyes took on a faraway expression. "You know what they say . . . 'When things are rough, hang in there or you'll never reach your full potential. Hardships make you stronger.'"

"That was beautiful," Herman said solemnly.

My little cup of joy overflowed with what Todd said next.

"I may be your god, but I'm also your *friend.* You don't ever have to be afraid of me."

I glanced at Herman, who had the thoughtful look he gets when he is about to issue a quote. "'There is nothing on this earth more to be prized than true friendship.'" He nodded at me. "Thomas Aquinas."

"Good one, Herman," Todd said, as he rose from his bed and crossed to his desk. He reached up and took a green plastic boat from the shelf that held his *Dragon Sensei* figures. "And as a token of my unchanging friendship and affection, I present you with General Ribbotti's boat, *The Ribbonator.*"

The boat was exquisite. It was fashioned out of a green lily pad, and the sail was an open white lotus flower. Herman was too overcome to say more than "We must show this to the others. Great Todd?"

Todd carried us to Toddlandia and presented the gift to the rest of his people. He offered them an eloquent apology for his recent neglect, the end of which was drowned out by our cheers.

While the others admired *The Ribbonator*, I asked Todd for a private word with him.

"Sure, Lewis," he said, placing me on his dresser. "What is it?"

I looked earnestly into Todd's face. "Could you take

off those glasses for a moment?" His eyebrows shot up, but he removed the glasses. "Do you seriously believe that . . . about hardships being sent our way to make us stronger?"

"Yeah, I do . . ." he said, his voice trailing off and his eyes widening. He chewed his bottom lip for a moment and knit his brows.

"Todd?" I said. "Is something wrong?"

He took a deep breath and heaved his shoulders. "No. Well, sort of . . ." He looked at me and said quickly, "But not with you. There's just something hard I have to do tonight . . . at the dance."

Now I took a deep breath and asked what was truly in my heart. "Did you really mean what you said a few moments ago? About us being friends?"

Todd grinned. "Absolutely." I could see my reflection shining in his dark pupils. "You and I will *always* be friends, Lew. I promise."

The doorbell rang then, which saved me from making a blubbering fool of myself. Todd placed me in my old spot on his shoulder, and we walked to the door.

He opened it. Lucy and Duddy stood on the stoop, looking exceptionally dapper in coordinating red and black ensembles. Todd nodded appreciatively and welcomed his friends inside. Duddy wore a black tie spangled with red chili peppers that I found quite aesthetically pleasing. Lucy's blouse was made of the same material, paired with a shiny black skirt; she explained that Susan had made them especially for the occasion.

"You're coming, aren't you, Todd?" Duddy asked, his voice high and unsure.

Lucy nodded. "You know it won't be nearly as much fun without you and your . . . break-dancing skills." She raised her eyebrows significantly. "So, what's it gonna be, Butroche?"

Todd smiled. "Of course I'm going." His friends' faces lit up. "But we need to stop by Charity's and pick her up first."

When we'd first returned from the river rescue, Todd had changed into khaki slacks and a denim button-down shirt, and he looked quite dashing. He invited his friends back to his bedroom so Lucy could assist him with the bright pink tie Duddy pulled from his pocket.

"Where did you get this?" Todd asked.

Duddy grinned. "A certain lovely young lady asked me to deliver it to you, and to tell you she *really* hoped you were going. I tried to tell her pink wasn't your color."

"It's fuchsia, actually," Todd replied. He had an odd expression as he looked down at the tie—almost as though he suspected it might bite him.

I watched from his shoulder as Lucy's nimble fingers made a neat knot in the tie. Heat was radiating off Todd's cheek, and Lucy's looked flushed as well.

"Are you coming with us?" Todd asked me. "You know you love 'festive occasions.'"

I yawned. "True, but tonight Lewis is just too pooped to party. I need to rest after this afternoon, which was an epic adventure."

Todd laughed and set me inside the fluffy slipper bed. "Sweet dreams, then, Lew."

I sighed and snuggled down into the familiar warmth of my own bed, at peace in the knowledge that I could count on Todd to return.

CHAPTER 25

I walked into the community center expecting to see kids slow dancing under a disco ball and couples kissing in corners. But the scene was completely different than I'd imagined, thank goodness.

There were a lot of people I didn't recognize, since the dance was open to other middle schools. But the guys, at least, had one thing in common: they were all huddled by the left wall under a giant paper spider on an orange streamer web. As Persephone would've put it, it looked like they'd "circled the wagons" in case any of the girls made a sneak attack from the other side of the big gym.

While the boys were joking and goofing off, the girls did in fact look like they were scheming how best to break the boys' ranks. They giggled and whispered by the punch bowl, pointing at the opposite sex like they were monkeys in a zoo.

As far as dancing, the floor was an empty no-man's-land. There *was* a disco ball shooting dots of white light all over the walls and floor, and the DJ practically begged somebody to come boogie. He even played that song that goes, "You make me wanna shout . . ." But it seemed he had the wrong crowd.

Lucy really didn't know any of the girls, and Charity—who looked jaw-droppingly gorgeous, of course—had pretty much superglued herself to my side, so Duddy and I strolled over to check out the grub table, girls in tow.

There was a big bowl of orange sherbet punch in the center of the table, and I started to help myself when Duddy asked Lucy if she would like "some refreshment." I followed his lead and gave Charity the cup I'd been pouring, then poured my own. That's when I heard Ike talking. It sounded like he was right under the table!

Ike was saying, "A little higher, now over to the right . . . Wait, stop! That's perfect! Very nice, Carmen."

A girl giggled, and then I heard Wendell's voice: "You think that's something? Watch us!"

Against my better judgment, I lifted the orange table-cloth to see what in the world they were doing under there.

Wendell, Ike, and their dates were lined up on their knees, building two pyramids out of clear plastic punch cups.

"Oh, hey, Todd!" Ike said, jumping up and clocking his head on the table. He rubbed his head and asked, "Whaddya think? Ours is the best, right?"

Before I could answer, Wendell made introductions. "Hail, noble warrior!" he said, bowing. "Alyssa and Carmen, this is Duddy's savior and fellow *Dragon Sensei* enthusiast, Todd Butroche." The girls, who looked surprisingly normal, grinned at me and giggled some more.

Duddy must have heard his name mentioned, because he looked under the table then, and so did Lucy and Charity. There were introductions all around. We couldn't persuade Ike and Wendell to come out and join the party yet; they had to have a timed "stack-off" first. It seemed they'd been only practicing.

"Was Wendell wearing a *kimono*?" Charity asked me as we filled our plates with snacks.

I smiled. "Actually, I think it was probably his mom's robe. Those two are a little strange at first, but once you get to know them, they're pretty great. Wendell has the most epic *Dragon Sensei* T-shirt collection of all time, and Ike . . . well, you saw his Mongee-Poo imitation at swim-team tryouts. He's hilarious."

Lucy had been listening. "Speaking of swim team," she said, piling grinning jack-o'-lantern sugar cookies on her plate, "in all the excitement earlier I completely forgot to ask you: How'd your meet go?"

Charity answered for me. "You guys should have seen

Todd! He blew everybody out of the water, almost literally, in all his heats! Earned the individual overall high score, too!" She looked at my chest. "Hey! You didn't wear your medal."

My ears burned, and I held up my pink tie. "I thought it might clash." That's when I noticed Lucy gawping at me and shaking her head. "What, Lucy?"

She let out a little laugh. "Todd, that's unbelievable! Why didn't you tell me? Last I heard you were going to quit the team!"

I shrugged and tossed a piece of candy corn into the air, catching it between my teeth. "Why would I do that?" Lucy opened her mouth, and I tossed one to her. She missed and turned to throw one to Duddy, but he was busy doing his classic "stuff Cheetos in your nose and pretend they're boogers" trick. I laughed, and the girls rolled their eyes.

Lucy dusted the Cheeto shrapnel off Duddy's vest. "I've got a joke for you guys: What is the show cesium and iodine love watching together?"

Duddy yanked the Cheetos out of his nostrils. He popped one in his mouth and said, "Uh . . . *The Science Guy*?"

Lucy smiled. "Good guess, Duddy. But the answer is C . . . S . . . I." She emphasized every letter and then snort-laughed. Charity and I chuckled politely; only Duddy admitted he didn't get it. Lucy started to explain, and then said, "Wait. Duddy, did you actually just *eat* that Cheeto?"

He blushed and changed the subject with another joke. "What's worse than finding a worm in your apple?"

"FINDING HALF A WORM," the three of us chorused.

"Duddy," I said, straightening my tie, "leave this to the professionals. What was the last thing that went through the grasshopper's mind when he hit the windshield?"

"HIS BUTT!" Duddy, Lucy, and Charity said at once.

"Amateurs," Charity bragged. "But back to worms: What's invisible and smells like worms?"

Finally, a stumper! We thought a minute, and then Duddy blurted, "Invisible worms?"

"Bird flatulence!" Lucy shouted. "My turn now! I know you boys will appreciate this one: If the Silver Surfer and Iron Man teamed up, what would they be?" She wriggled her eyebrows and took a sip of punch.

I looked at Duddy, who shrugged and said, "Un-stoppable?"

"They'd be *alloys,* get it?"

We didn't.

"You know, instead of 'allies,' 'alloys'—it's where you mix an inferior metal with a more precious one."

I stuffed a marshmallow ghost thingy into my mouth and nodded. Duddy, however, laughed like it was the funniest joke he'd ever heard. "Alloys! Oh, that's a good one! *Alloys.*"

Man, he had it for her *bad.*

Charity went to "refresh herself," and Duddy followed her, saying he had "urgent business" to take care of.

Lucy chewed her cheek the way she does when she's about to say something serious. "Todd, have you given any more consideration to letting me set up a webcam in your room? After today's events, I just feel like the Toddlians need some extra surveillance and protection."

"I don't think that would be a good idea, Lucy. I mean, a guy has to have his privacy." My ears burned even more, but at least I'd finally said it. "And besides, I swear to you, I'm going to be taking a lot better care of the Toddlians from here on out. I just got temporarily . . . distracted."

"Yeah, right," she said, smiling. "You just don't want me to catch you break-dancing in your boxers or something."

She was right about that. Her face lit up, and mine did, too, for some reason.

The lights dimmed then, and the DJ said in a low, creepy voice, "All right, young bucks, grab your gal pal by the hand and let's slow it down a little. C'mon now, don't be shy."

A romantic song started to play, and Charity crossed the floor and walked up to me, grabbing my hand. "Oooo, this one's my favorite!" She turned on the eyelashes and said, "Will you dance with me, Todd?"

Had something happened to the air conditioning? Why had it suddenly gotten so hot? None of the other guys apparently had the guts to walk across the room and grab their "gal pal" by the hand. I already had that step down.

After all I'd been through today, I felt up to anything. "Sure," I said, smiling. "Let's show 'em how it's done."

That was pretty stupid of me to say, since I'd never actually danced with another person before. Everyone was staring at us.

But then it hit me: I, Todd Butroche, certified dork, was about to dance with the prettiest girl in the room. "What do we do now?" I whispered once we were under the disco ball.

She put my hands around her waist and then put hers on my shoulders. We swayed slowly in a circle. "See, it's easy," she said.

If I was hot before, I was now at lava level. I kind of wiped my sweaty hands on her dress, and I guess she must've thought I was getting cuddly, because she stepped closer and laid her head on my shoulder. *Can she hear how fast my heart is beating?* I looked forward, trying not to get dizzy from the swirling smells of her flowery perfume and her tropical shampoo.

Suddenly Charity leaned toward my face. Her eyelids slid closed, and her lips parted . . . I stared at her glossy pink lips and went all woozy. *She wants me to kiss her!*

I tensed and stopped swaying. It should have been my dream come true, but instead, this felt like too much. My body was sending my brain all kinds of signals that I just didn't want to deal with yet. Other guys could do what they wanted, but I still liked feeling in charge of my feelings.

I cleared my throat. *What did I just tell the Toddlians? It's worth it to do the hard things . . .*

"What's wrong?" Charity asked, raising her head.

"This," I said, stepping away from her. Her eyes widened, and I tried to say the next part as gently as I could. "Charity, you are *so* cool, and I really, really like you. But I'm not ready . . . for *this*. Does that make sense?"

She just looked at me for a few seconds, like she didn't believe me. Then she slowly nodded, lowering her eyes. I felt my gut clench. *Please don't cry.* I bent my knees and looked up into her face. "Hey, we're still friends, right?" I gave her a mini Saki Salute, and she smiled.

"O-of course, Todd. We still have to have our *Dragon Sensei* battle jam in which I whip your and Duddy's butts, remember?"

I laughed as oceans of relief rolled over me. We started dancing again, talking out the logistics of our battle jam. She was determined to get Lucy to join us in her Vespa costume. I didn't say it, but I thought it would be supercool if they became friends, too.

"Hey, look at that!" I said as Duddy led Lucy to the dance floor. Their faces were both bright pink, and they were giggling like crazy people.

"We're trendsetters," Charity said, nodding toward Cassandra, who was—*carrying Ernie over her shoulder?* She set him down on the dance floor, and it was hard not to stare. Ernie circled her on tiptoe while she rotated in place with her arms around his neck.

While I was gawking at the redheaded lovebirds, someone tore Charity out of my arms. I whipped around to see Max in jeans and a black satin tuxedo jacket. Under the jacket he wore a skull-and-roses Ed Hardy T-shirt. He'd actually combed his hair, and it was slicked into a swoopy Elvis 'do.

"Don't mind if I cut in, do you, Buttrock?"

"It looks like *she* does." I said, as Charity struggled to wrench her hand out of Max's grip.

He glared at me, then said with mock sympathy, "I'm so sorry to hear about the loss of your little buggy buddies. You must be brokenhearted."

He stuck his bottom lip out in a fake pout, and I wanted to punch it. But instead I said, "Actually, they've never been better, no thanks to you."

Max looked confused and must've relaxed his grip because Charity got away from him, giving him a shove in the chest for good measure. She shook her finger in his face. "You listen to me, Max Loving, and get this straight."

The other couples who had come out on the floor stopped dancing and watched. Even the music paused as the DJ, taking in the show, seemed to forget to put on the next song.

"I do *not like you.* I've never liked you, and I never will. Furthermore, I don't appreciate being manhandled and fought over like some pretty little toy or . . . or tasty pastry or something."

Max jerked his head toward me but looked at her. "This is all about *him*, isn't it? If it weren't for him—"

Charity crossed her arms and tossed her hair. "At least Todd knows how to treat a girl with a little respect. Ever heard of it? This has nothing to do with Todd besting you. I wouldn't go out with you if you were the only guy on the planet." She turned and sashayed to the girls' room.

"Sing it, sister!" Lucy yelled.

Max's shoulders slumped, and for a brief moment I saw a softness in his face that was completely un-Max-like. He sighed and stared at his sneakers while the DJ seemed to get his act together and everybody else started doing the "YMCA."

He was clearly in a weakened state. This was my chance to put a stop to his threats once and for all. I took a power stance in front of him. "Max, you'd better steer clear of me and the Toddlians from now on, and I mean it."

His eyes met mine, the old fire back in them. "Or *what*?"

"Or . . ." I hadn't thought this far ahead, so I said the first thing that popped into my brain. "Or I've got a sur- veillance camera over my garage with some real interest- ing footage of your epic wipeout on my skateboard. That wipeout already kinda ruined your reputation with Spud and those guys, didn't it?" I leaned in close, whispering right into Max's reddening face. "Who knows what dam- age would be done if even more people found out?"

He was morphing into Hulk-Max mode as I spoke. Angry unibrow, nostrils flared, flexed muscles, the whole routine. "I don't need Spud and Dick, loser. And if you think I believe that story for one second, you're even stupider than I thought. Surveillance camera, huh!" He snorted and leaned over me. "You really think I'm an idiot, don't you, bug boy?"

I didn't flinch. "All right, tough guy. Why don't you come to my house after the dance and check it out, then?"

He stared at me, not moving. He didn't know what to do.

I glared up at him. "I'd hate to have to show that video to Charity, because I'm sure she'd show it to all her friends. And you know how YouTube works, right? Within a week every girl in the country will have seen 'Max Meets Driveway.'"

I raised my eyebrows and pressed my lips together. "Now *that* could be embarrassing. I mean, we know Charity doesn't like you. But that would kind of zap your chances with every girl in school, huh?" I looked at Max. He looked somehow smaller than he had a minute before. "So you better leave my 'little bug people' alone. *Comprende?*"

Max stepped back and twitched his head to one side. "All right, Buttrock." He gave my shoulder a parting shove. "You win this round. You and I could probably use a break from each other, anyway."

He started to slink off toward the exit, but I stopped

him. I was still curious about something. "Hey, Loving!"
Max turned toward me slowly. "What did you see in
Charity, anyway? It doesn't seem like the two of you have
anything in common."

Max glared at me. For a second, I thought I could
actually see pain in his eyes, but then they hardened.
"What did I see in Charity?" he asked. "A pulse and two
X chromosomes, that's all! I thought she might be cool,
but . . . *clearly* she's not, if she's into you." He whipped
his head around, looking all over the dance floor. "YOU
HEAR THAT, LADIES?" he yelled. "THIS IS YOUR LUCKY
NIGHT, BECAUSE MAX LOVING IS BACK ON THE
MARKET!" He flexed his meaty biceps, gave a quick nod,
and then turned, weaving in and out of YMCAers toward
the door.

I mean, obviously he was lying. I knew Max, and I
knew he wouldn't have put so much effort into wooing
Charity if he didn't actually like her. But it was silly of me
to think he'd ever tell me, or anyone, what he was really
feeling.

For just a second, I felt sorry for him. But then a vision
of him pushing the Toddlians down the sewer drain
flashed before my eyes, and I got over my sympathy pains
real quick.

*Max is right, for once. It's time we take a break from
each other.*

CHAPTER 26

All that confrontation had made me thirsty, and I strolled back over to the punch bowl for a hit of orange-sherbet sweetness. Lucy and Duddy were lining up to do the limbo, and when Lucy saw me, she whispered something to Duddy and headed in my direction.

"Hey, Todd!" she said, pouring herself some punch. "What exactly happened back there?"

I shrugged. "Nothing big. But I don't think Max will be bothering us anymore. Or the Toddlians."

"Oh, good." Lucy drained her cup, smiling with a funny foam mustache. "So much heavenly refined sugar! But that's not what I meant. What happened before that, with Charity?"

"Oh." I guzzled my punch and wiped my mouth with a black napkin. I folded it up into fourths as I talked. "I, uh . . . I told her that I wasn't ready for all this boy-girl stuff and that I thought we should just be friends."

I looked at her then, and her dark eyes were big and sparkly. It could have been the sugar; I dunno.

"I'm glad you feel that way, Todd. Like I said the other night, we're too young for dating. Friendship is good. For now."

Duddy had walked up behind her, and by the devastated look on his face, I knew he'd heard us. But nothing could keep the Dudster down for long. "Yeah, we're pretty lucky to have each other as friends," he said, nodding like he was convincing himself. "Right? I mean, you don't find a trifecta of coolness like this every day!"

Lucy laughed. "Hey, fellas, whaddaya say we blow this Popsicle stand? I've had about all the Katy Perry and high-fructose corn syrup I can stomach. And these stupid stilts mislabeled as shoes!" She pulled a pinched-up foot out of a red heel and picked it up. "These are so structurally flawed. Throws you completely off balance and causes you to lean forward at a precarious angle, not to mention the punishment to your arches . . ." Our eyes must have been glazing over, because she said, "Anyway, you guys ready to go?"

"Absolutely!" I jogged over to Charity, who was sitting in a folding chair and chatting with Ernie and Cassandra about the basics of badminton. "We're going back to my house to hang out for a while. You in?"

Charity smiled. "Aw, thanks for asking me, Todd. But I told E and C here that I'd go with them to watch some of their *Badminton for Beginners* DVDs. I can't go out for it this year because of swim team, but I've always wanted to learn. Maybe we can all get together and play sometime."

I glanced at Cassandra, who was trading retainers with Ernie. He had Batman on his, and she had Hello Kitty on hers.

"Uh, yeah, sure. That'd be great!" I headed back to my gang feeling kind of relieved that Charity wasn't coming. Now I could bring out the Toddlians!

Back at my house we warmed up some sweat "à la Todd Bod" (as Herman called it) for the little dudes and some hot chocolate for Duddy and me. Lucy drank water. "I don't want to go into a sugar coma or anything," she explained.

While we had been at the dance the Toddlians had planned a little surprise. We gathered outside my closet and knelt down beside Toddlandia to see what it was, passing the micro-glasses back and forth so we wouldn't miss anything.

Lewis asked me to fill a giant bowl with water, and I did as he asked and placed it on the closet floor. Then Herman had the Toddlians board *The Ribbonator*. The Toddlians wanted to give the boat a new name, but Herman was worried that if it wasn't renamed properly, they might "incur the wrath of some evil demigod." I thought he was probably talking about Daisy, and I promised him that she didn't even know they existed. He looked at me funny and asked to proceed with the ceremony.

"Are you all aboard?" I asked, gently setting the boat on the water.

"Darn tootin'!" Persephone hollered. "Let's get this done; I'm feelin' greener than a garter snake with the grippe."

Something tickled my hand. It was Lewis, climbing up my finger. "Great—I mean, Just Plain Todd," he said, skittering up my arm to my shoulder, "may I watch the ceremony from up here? Recent unpleasant events are still too fresh in my memory to desire a boat ride at present."

"Sure," I said. "Best seat in the house."

Herman addressed us from the bow. "My friends, we gather here today to christen this vessel with a new name, worthy of her beauty and watertightness."

The Toddlians cheered, and we joined in.

"Ships have watched faithfully over sailors for thousands of years, the way a mother does her wee babe, and therefore, we lovingly refer to them as 'she.' Now raise your cups and join me in a toast. To the sailors of yore! To *The Butroche*!"

"TO THE SAILORS OF YORE!" we cried. "TO *THE BUTROCHE*!"

Everybody took a sip, except me. My jaw dropped, and then I couldn't stop smiling.

"That's so cool!" Duddy said.

"With all due respect, gentlemen," Herman said solemnly. "Please do not interrupt the christening ceremony. We must do this hastily, before any evil spirits become aware of our proceedings."

He cleared his throat. "The moods of Dais—waves are unstable. But the keel of this ship is sturdy and will carry us safely to harbor on every voyage. Let us toast: TO THE WIND AND THE WAVES! TO *THE BUTROCHE*!"

We repeated the toast and took another sip.

"And finally," Herman said, choking up a bit, "to our only god, who saved his people out of the raging river, who built this remarkable city for us to dwell in, and who treats us not as slaves but as friends. Today we formally reaffirm our loyalty to you. TO GREAT TODD! AND TO *THE BUTROCHE*!"

"TO GREAT TODD! AND TO *THE BUTROCHE*!"

Lucy sniffled, and I might have, too. She poured a cup of sweat over the bow and proclaimed, "Today we name this lady *The Butroche*! May your waters always be calm, may your voyages be prosperous, and may you Toddlians never know fear again, in any of its forms."

"TO THE TODDLIANS!" I cried, raising my mug.

Duddy and Lucy joined me. "TO THE TODDLIANS!"

Herman led us in the Toddlandian anthem, and we

cheered so loud Mom popped her head in the door. "You might want to keep it down—Daisy's asleep."

I pulled off my glasses and jumped up to block her view. "We'll settle down, I promise."

She shut the door, and then opened it again. "Oh, Todd! I forgot to tell you; Daisy said your name today! She very distinctly said, 'Todd.'"

"That's awesome!"

Mom nodded. "I thought you'd like to know. But then she said another name; I think it must be one of the babies from her playdate. Right after she said 'Todd,' she said, 'Lee Ann,' as clear as a bell. Crazy, huh? You guys have fun!"

Todd, Lee Ann? Huh. Is there a Lee Ann in her playgroup? I didn't remember one from when they met here and I'd had to help . . . But how cool that Daisy'd finally learned my name!

I went to sleep that night with Lewis snuggled into my pillow, just like old times. He yawned and said, "Pleasant dreams, Todd."

I held out my finger. "You too, Lew. High five?"

Lewis jumped up and smacked my finger, then nuzzled back into my pillow. He sighed and said, "It's so nice having a god who cares for you. But it's even nicer having that god for your friend."

I smiled into the darkness. "You got that right, compadre. Friends *are* good . . . of every size."

ACKNOWLEDGMENTS:

THE AUTHOR WOULD LIKE TO THANK: *The One who is always faithful; Bobby, for dreaming with me; my children, for being my encouragement posse; Ben and Gillian, for giving me this amazing opportunity; Stephanie, Elizabeth, and Lynn, for their kind and wise words; Patrick, for breathing life into these characters with your incredible illustrations; Lis, for being the world's most supportive sister; Lisa, for her devotion not only to my work, but to the children of our community; to my fellow OneFours, whose camaraderie I cherish; Matthew, for his anime expertise and playing Koi Boy without complaining; and Jay, Nic, Frank, Lu, Amy, Deanna, Mike, Shellie, Amber, and Richard, for being there from the get-go.*